UNCLE PINK

Dirt-n-All

Bill Winn

TWS | The Writer's Society Publishing

To request permissions, contact TWS Publishing at www.thewriterssociety.online

Paperback: ISBN 978-1-961180-27-7

TWS Publishing
Lodi, CA
www.thewriterssociety.online

To my wife Davina, A dream is little more than fantasy if never realized. This work is not that. This book is merely a happy accident borne in the miracle of my truest dream... marrying you.

Contents

Preface

Love is a simple concept. Loving people is not. Some are easier to love than others. Some are more practiced in showing love, while others are better at receiving and believing love.

When someone, who desperately needs love, is blessed or fortunate enough to land in a place where people have mastered the art of pouring out undiluted love and acceptance, beautiful things are possible.

The Malone family in Paige County, Virginia was a simple farm family that was well practiced at demonstrating other-centered love. Theirs was not a perfect family, but it was a good one.

We all belong to love but the Malones had discovered the rich treasures of living as though it were true. Genuine love always has room for more.

The Malone family's love seemed vastly limitless.

In the winter of 1914, a little lost boy would put that love to the test.

I invite you to come read a tale of loss, love, redemption, mischief and laughter.

It is my hope that you will find in this book simple goodness and pure joy.

Bill Winn

P.S. If you are reading this book for the first time, you are enjoying a gift I did not give to my close friends and family. For them, they read the book a chapter or two at a time as I wrote.

Benjamin Franklin once said, "Never ruin an apology with an excuse."

I would like to say to all my friends and family, to whom I sent chapters to read, that I am truly sorry if I robbed you of the full experience of this story... it's just that I get so excited and I love you all so much I couldn't help it.

Chapter 1

Little Man

C *lick clack, click clack, click clack...* the rhythm of the train's wheels moving over the tracks was a drone that had put most of the stowaways and hobos to sleep. There were about twenty-five or thirty people in the empty livestock car. In the back, far away from the door, a middle-aged man and woman were trying to get some rest. The man was about forty years old. His face wore more wrinkles than most his age. There was a little boy with the couple, and he was pestering them because he needed to relieve himself.

"Pee-pee," pleaded the boy.

"You can hold it," grunted the man in reply.

The smell of whiskey on him was pungent. The stench offended the child's nose, and he pinched his nostrils together in protest. The man kicked at the boy, but he was quicker and moved out of reach. A little while later, the child returned and tried to shake the woman awake. He tugged at her jacket. "Accident," said the boy. Groggy from a drunken stupor and her sleep, the woman sat up. "What!" she snapped. Repeating himself and whimpering the boy said, "Accident." Moonlight blinked in and out of the open boxcar door as the train passed hills and trees. The pulsing light slowed as the train approached a whistle stop to take on fuel and water. Moonlight flashed on the child, and the woman could see that he'd wet himself.

"You little bastard!" she shouted.

"I'm sorry," he sobbed.

She lunged at the boy, her face distorted with anger and hatred, "C'mere!" The child ducked her hand and ran through the crowded car. She got up and kicked the man to wake him.

"What, what is it?" he barked.

"That little runt ran off— is what!" she shouted.

The man growled in reply, "Well, dammit! Find him! We can't score without him."

After making a half-hearted effort to find him, the woman gave up. She muttered something under her breath and shuffled back over to her companion, spitting on the floor in disgust. The boy would be somebody else's problem now.

She sat on the boxcar floor, next to the man and poked him in the back. "He's run off," she hissed, "and I can't find him."

"Fine, let the dogs have him," he replied and rolled back over, pulling his hat down over his face.

When the train stopped, crews of men began to fill the engine's water tank and take on more fuel for the coal car. A few of the stowaways got off, and a few more got on. Desperate to get away from the drunken angry couple, the boy climbed down off the train and disappeared.

It was a cold November night. The moon ducked in and out of clouds that had been drizzling half-frozen droplets for days. The raindrops stung the boy's face, as if mocking his already cold cheeks. He wrapped his arms tightly around himself and shuddered. He was free from the anger, hatred, and abuse, but freedom had come at a price. The cost of his liberation was cold, hunger, and darkness. He was alone.

"Thank you kindly, Mr. Yoder," said Warner stepping up onto the buckboard.

Edward was loading the last of the flour and salt onto the wagon. He waved to Mr. Yoder and climbed onto the seat next to his father.

"Get up!" Warner commanded. Molly and Alice obediently began to pull the wagon up the street. Neither of Warner's two horses would have won any contests for speed or beauty, but they did everything he needed them to do. They could pull a wagon, or a plow, or drag logs out of the woods for lumber and firewood. In a strictly utilitarian sense, they were perfect.

Edward pulled the collar on his wool coat up to cover his ears. "Mighty raw out tonight," he shouted over the noise of the hoof beats and the rattle of the old wagon.

"Maybe your mama will have a pot of hot coffee on the stove when we get home. That'll warm up your innards," laughed Warner.

Edward shook his head acknowledging his daddy. The pair rode on for about ten minutes more, when Edward spied something on the path. At first glance, he thought it to be some sort of animal, but then he called out, "Stop, there's a baby in the road!"

Warner pulled the reins taught and shouted, "Whoa!" Molly and Alice came to a stop and whinnied in protest.

There in front of them, staring emotionless was a little boy near about four years of age. He was alone and had nothing on but an old pair of shoes, trousers, and a long-sleeved shirt. He had no coat, no hat, and no socks. His hair was long, blond, and tangled. His face was dirty, his lips chapped, and his trousers wet. He was a pitiful sight.

Jumping down off the wagon Warner asked, "What'll we do with him?"

"Do with him!" exclaimed Edward. "Why do we have to do something with him? Where's his ma and pa? Mama's gonna be fit to be tied if we bring home another mouth to feed," he added.

"I don't know where his folks are, but we can't leave him here. And you let me worry about your mother," he said smiling. "It's bitter cold out and the poor fella ain't even got a coat on."

He scanned up and down the road to see if anyone was near and called out, "Hello! Is anybody out there?" No answer came. It was too dark to see and too cold to linger. The wind stiffened and blew back the boy's tangled locks. Standing with his arms wrapped tightly around himself to preserve as much warmth as possible, he looked up at Warner and Edward but did not speak. His face had no tell of emotion. He was expressionless.

"He's awful pitiful, ain't he Daddy? I wonder who he belongs to or where he came from," Edward mused.

"You got a name little man?" Warner asked the boy.

Nodding his head in the affirmative, but not speaking, the boy began crying softly. Tears streaked down his little face, and he lowered his head. He was well-trained in manipulating hearts.

Warner turned to Edward with a panicked hurt on his face. "Let's get him in the wagon." He scooped the boy into his arms, with no protest from the child. Any fight in him that would have prevented Warner from picking him up, had been swallowed up by hunger and cold. Warner stepped up onto the wagon and handed the child to his son. Edward did his best to wrap him inside his coat, for it was bitterly cold.

Warner shouted, "Get up!" as he picked up the reins. The two-horse team started at a walk, before getting up to a steady trot. The springs on the wagon seat gave just enough relief from the rutted old road to make their speed tolerable. Just a few minutes into the trip home, resting against Edward's shoulder, the boy fell asleep.

"When we get home I want you to draw some water for the kettle. We'll need to get something warm in his belly for him to sleep on—something besides coffee," said Warner.

"Alright daddy, I'll bring in some extra stove wood to keep the house warm all night too," offered Edward.

It's in moments of need—especially urgent need—tucked in the space between words that the Lord so often whispers to his children, and we would be wise to listen carefully.

The preacher's words came back to Warner, and he thought to himself that once again the timing was impeccable. He looked over at Edward and the child, and said, "Between here and home say a prayer for us. We'll need the Lord's wisdom in full measure I expect."

Edward nodded and smiled. The Malone family wasn't very religious in the way that some folks are, but they loved the Lord and tried hard to live like it.

When they arrived at the Malone farm, Warner stopped the wagon in front of the house and took the boy from Edward. Stirring awake, the boy shivered so violently that Warner nearly lost hold of him.

"I know," said Warner, "Jack Frost will have all our noses if we don't get inside by the fire."

Chapter 2

Can We Keep Him

E dward opened the door and Warner stepped inside carrying the boy.

"What on earth!" exclaimed Mary Ethel.

"It's a child," replied Warner.

"I can see that," she replied. "Where ever did he come from?"

"Mama, we don't know, we just found him wanderin' up the road," explained Edward.

Mary Ethel reached out, took the child from Warner, and held him close. She rubbed her hand vigorously up and down his back in an attempt to warm him.

"Come child, let's get you by the stove," she said.

Warner grabbed a rocking chair from the front room and pulled it into the kitchen next to the pot-bellied wood stove. The boy stared emotionless at the Malones. He made no sound as he sat on Mary Ethel's lap. There was a lot to take in. The

Malone household was full of life and all the fuss over him was almost more than the boy could manage.

Edward made silly faces at the child and reached a finger out to tickle him, but the boy recoiled. Edward reflexively withdrew his hand and gave his daddy a quizzical look.

Warner nodded in understanding and said, "Maybe little man is too tired to play right now." He smiled at the boy but got no reaction from him.

Retrieving a cold biscuit from the pie safe, Edward held it out to the boy. He took it reluctantly and ate it too quickly for Mary Ethel's liking.

"Have mercy," she exclaimed, "I've seen hounds eat slower!"

Warner walked over, knelt next to the chair, and gave the child a wooden cup half-full of warmed milk.

"You drink this up now son," Warner said grinning, "and you'll grow as big and strong as a mule."

Taking the cup in both hands, he sipped the milk slower than he'd eaten the biscuit. When he'd finished the milk, he handed the cup back to Warner, who placed it on the counter.

Mary Ethel cradled the child's head against her shoulder and said, "Edward, fetch me a quilt, a good heavy one. This baby feels like he's cold all the way through to his bones."

Just then, Victoria came down the stairs with a book in her hand. "What's all the fuss?" she inquired.

Edward interrupted, "Vicky, mama said go fetch a good warm quilt."

"We have a special visitor," added Mary Ethel.

"Oh, mama, a baby! Can we keep him?" asked Vicky with excitement.

"He's a child, not a stray dog!" scolded Edward.

"Of course, of course," reassured Vicky, "I just meant are we going to give him a home?"

"I expect he's already got a home, Victoria. In the morning, I'll carry him to the sheriff. He'll know better how to find out where he came from and where he belongs, but for tonight we need to get him fed up and warmed up, so go get that quilt like your mama asked," replied Warner.

Edward grinned at his mother in satisfaction at having passed his assignment on to his sister. Mary Ethel gave him a half-hearted scowl.

"I'm gonna go get in some stove wood," said Edward.

Warner followed him out the door saying, "I need to barn the horses, and let's not forget to get in an overnight log."

"Yes sir," replied Edward.

Victoria came back down the stairs holding a good warm quilt. It was thick and heavy, made from scraps of flour sacks and old clothes too tattered to mend. She stopped at the edge of the kitchen and watched her mother rocking the little boy. She felt an intense joy and smiled. Mary Ethel noticed her and returned the smile, she too had felt the same happiness. Vicky gave Mary Ethel the quilt and together they carefully wrapped the boy, tucking the blanket around his chilled body.

"Here," said Vicky picking up the boy's legs, "see if you can wrap up his feet, they must be near to frost bit." Her mother finished bundling the boy in the quilt and began rocking him to sleep.

"I'll go help Edward," said Vicky.

She stepped out into the moonlight and looked up at its

source. The world always seemed so small to her when she looked at the moon— she often wondered who in the wide world might, at that exact moment, be staring at it too. Such thoughts gave her peace and hope. But in this particular moment, she fretted about the mystery of the little boy's future and his past. She wondered if a heartbroken mother was somewhere frantically searching for her baby in the light of this same moon. Her imagination created tragedies and triumphs, while her heart ached for the poor waif.

Alone in the kitchen with the little boy, Mary Ethel found a comfortable rhythm in the rocking chair and began to sing to the child by the warmth of the wood stove.

"Golden slumbers kiss your eyes,
Smiles await you when you rise.
Sleep, Pretty baby, Do not cry,
And I will sing a lullaby."

Mary Ethel sang softly and it wasn't long before he fell asleep again. "You poor thing, you must be exhausted," whispered Mary Ethel. "Don't you worry none. You're gonna be just fine. The good Lord'll see to that."

Shortly, Edward came back inside with an armload of stove wood. His arms full, he pushed the door open with his foot. The door got away from him and slammed into the wall.

"Shhhhhhh!" hissed his mother.

"Sorry," whispered Edward.

Mary Ethel smiled and rolled her eyes. Still whispering,

Edward stacked the wood by the wall and said, "Sometimes I don't know my own strength."

Grinning his mother retorted, "It's because you belong to your daddy." Edward smiled, suppressing the urge to laugh.

Right behind Edward, Victoria and Warner both came in with a load of firewood. Warner was carrying a large round log that he would later place in the wood stove right before bed; to give the fire something to slowly consume all through the night.

"Mama, reckon we ought to bring the dogs in tonight?" asked Warner.

Mary Ethel replied, "Those dogs have slept out in the hay on nights much colder than this one."

"Sure they have," agreed Warner, "I mean for the boy."

"Oh, yes, indeed... that's a good idea. I'll make up a pallet here on the floor by the stove and the dogs can sleep in here next to him," said Mary Ethel.

"Two good size dogs, one on either side ought to keep him plenty warm," said Warner.

Mary Ethel watched as Warner led the dogs inside. Rusty and Jumper were visibly happy to be inside the warm house. They both walked over to Mary Ethel to sniff the newcomer. She stopped rocking as the dogs approached and let them each inspect the strange little visitor.

Almost no one in Paige County locked the doors to their homes. There simply wasn't any need, and besides a locked door only serves to slow a person down when they have to get to the outhouse in a hurry, in the middle of the night. But on this night, Warner thought it best to lock them, to keep the boy from wandering off.

Turning the key to lock the door, he wondered aloud, "If it turns out the little fella has no home, what do you reckon we should do? I mean, we can't just give him to the county, who knows who might end up with him and what may come of him."

Still rocking the child, Mary Ethel nodded and replied, "Best we pray on it right steady 'til we find out."

As Vicky made up the pallet, Edward got some milk from the ice box and poured it into a jar. Sipping the milk, he leaned against the kitchen counter and placed a hand on his hip. He stared at the boy and noticed how easily and peacefully he slept.

"It's past your bedtime Vicky," said Mary Ethel.

"Oh, mama, please let me stay up," she pleaded.

"There'll be enough to do for both of us come morning. I need you rested and up early tomorrow. Now off to bed with you," answered her mother.

Vicky gave her mother and father a kiss and reluctantly started up the stairs. She paused halfway up the steps and stooped to see back into the kitchen. She said a silent prayer for the boy, "Lord, keep that poor boy and help him know we mean only to help."

Edward finished his milk and put the cup on the kitchen table. Warner pointed at the sink. Edward, picking up the glass to place it in the sink, said, "Dad, what kind of mother would leave her youngin to wander off in the cold of winter?"

"I don't know son," he replied. "We ought not judge anyone. We don't know what might have happened, so just pray that his family is okay and we find them soon."

"His mama must be worried sick to death," added Mary Ethel. "I know I would be."

"Well, I'm going to get some sleep," said Edward. "I've had enough excitement for today." He kissed his mother and disappeared up the stairs.

As Mary Ethel rocked the boy, the chair sang its rickety lullaby. Strung together with squeaks, cricks, and pops the rhythm was steady, consistent, and familiar.

Warner looked at his beloved and reminisced, "It's been a while since we've sat together in this kitchen while you rocked a little one to sleep."

He reached over and stroked her hand. Mary Ethel stopped her rocking for a moment to take in the sincerity of his touch. The child shifted, still asleep, in protest. A smile beamed across her face and Mary Ethel picked up her rhythm again. It pleased her to know the boy appreciated her presence.

After a few more minutes, Mary Ethel ceased her rocking and studied the child closely for a reaction. When none came, she shifted to stand from the chair.

"Do you need some help putting him down?" asked Warner.

"I reckon I can manage. The poor thing can't weigh 30 pounds. I wonder when he last ate a full meal?" she replied. Mary Ethel carefully laid the child on the pallet between Rusty and Jumper, who had already made themselves at home on the blankets. She knelt down to kiss his rosy cheek and covered him with the quilt.

Warner extended a hand to help her up from the floor and Mary Ethel asked, "What time are you figuring to go see the sheriff? I want to see that you have something to eat before you go."

Pulling her to her feet, he kept his grip on her hand and pulled her into an embrace. "You're a remarkable woman Mary Ethel Malone," he whispered. She leaned back, smiled, and gave him a kiss. The pair stood in the kitchen watching the boy sleep for some time without speaking.

"Are you praying?" asked Mary Ethel.

"Yep." replied Warner, "My heart hurts for the little fella."

"There's no telling what he's seen or been through in his life," said Mary Ethel, "Tonight's events would be hard enough on anyone, especially a baby. I have to believe you found him for a reason."

"I'm sure it'll all become clear, by and by." Warner's words comforted Mary Ethel.

"Let's get to sleep darling. It's late," she said.

Warner opened the door on the wood stove and chucked in the big round overnight log. He groaned as he stood, and taking her hand, led Mary Ethel off to bed.

Chapter 3

Pink

The following morning, Warner awakened to an empty bed. He ran his arm around under the covers searching for his wife but she was absent. *"She must be up cooking already,"* he thought. Warner sipped from the glass of water on the night-stand and stood up to stretch. "Lord, I love you and I want today to be filled with goodness," he prayed. It was a rote prayer that he'd said for many years and had found that it set his mood right for the day's tasks that lay ahead. It was especially impor-tant today, because a little boy's fate depended on that goodness.

The situation troubled him greatly but Warner had done his best not to show signs of worry. "Fear and worry is catchin'," he'd often say.

Walking downstairs, Warner could see Mary Ethel asleep in the rocking chair holding the boy. Both wrapped in the quilt, they were fast asleep. He opened the door to the pot-bellied wood stove as quietly as possible and stoked the fire. The overnight log had performed well, leaving behind a nice bed of coals on the floor of the stove. He raked the coals into a pile and shoveled the loose ash into a tin pail.

Building the fire back up with a fresh load of oak, he closed the door. The sound of it closing stirred Mary Ethel awake. Warner looked at her and smiled.

"How long have you been down here with him?" he asked.

"Since about two this morning," she answered. "I heard him cry out in his sleep, and when I came down the stairs, he was standing in the middle of the floor crying."

"I rocked him to sleep again, and when I went to put him down, he jolted awake and held onto my neck for dear life." Mary Ethel, teary-eyed, added, "I couldn't... I wouldn't leave him."

"You're a good woman, Mary Ethel Malone. This child could not have done better than to land here in your lap," said Warner as he scooped grounds into the coffee pot.

She looked down at the sleeping child and said, "Oh, he's blessed to be in this house, not just in my lap. I'd be willing to bet that as soon as Vicky gets up, she'll dote on him every minute of the day. She's as generous with her heart as a child can be. I just hope she isn't too hurt when he goes home to his family."

Warner grabbed a few biscuits and placed them on the top of the woodstove to warm while the coffee was brewing.

"Were you warm enough last night?" he asked. "Plenty," replied Mary Ethel. "Warner, I felt something in this boy's chest last night."

There was a worried tone in her voice. Curious, Warner replied, "Oh?"

"Yes, it's like every so often, his heart skips a beat or two," she explained.

Warner fiddled with the coffee pot and turned the biscuits over. Her concerned tone of voice was familiar. He knew she was investing her feelings in the boy. It would have been strange to him had she not, but still, the child wasn't theirs, and a parting would be soon upon them. He hated the thought of her heart being broken.

"I'm sure it's just the stress of last night and being lost from his family, not to mention being in a strange home with even stranger folks," he said with a chuckle. He tried his best to ease Mary Ethel's concern, but looking over his shoulder he noticed her worried expression had not changed.

Acknowledging that his distraction hadn't worked, Warner offered, "Maybe I can take the child with me into town and after I see the sheriff, I can go by Doc Webber's and let him have a look at the little fella. It's Saturday, so maybe he's at home."

"I reckon you'd best let me ride along and mind him while you drive the wagon," instructed Mary Ethel.

"Well, you'll want more on than a nightgown I'd wager," laughed Warner.

Mary Ethel rolled her eyes and motioned to shoo him away. By now the child was awake and eating a biscuit. Warner cut him a slice of ham from the icebox and he ate it with the same enthusiasm as before.

Mary Ethel got up and set the boy on the rocking chair while she excused herself to clean up and dress to go out.

"You need to visit the Johnny house young man?" Warner asked. The boy did not speak, but nodded his head. Warner scooped him from the chair and toted him to the outhouse. The morning was brisk but it wasn't cold. It wasn't nearly as cold as the night before, and the drizzling rain had finally stopped.

Rusty and Jumper eagerly followed Warner and the boy out the door. They got to work straight away re-marking trees and bushes to ensure that whatever critters might venture into the yard would know whose territory it was.

Taking the boy into the outhouse, Warner helped him with his britches. Pulling the child's trousers down, he could see bruises of different shades all over his buttocks and legs. *"Dear Lord!"* he thought. When the boy finished, Warner helped him clean up and pull up his pants. He knew he'd have to tell what he'd seen. He had no qualms about telling the sheriff and the doctor, it was Mary Ethel that he dreaded telling. He knew it would grieve her to know the boy had been beaten.

Bringing the child back inside the house, he set him on the floor. The child just stood, as before, emotionless, and surveyed the room. It was light enough now that he could see into the front room of the house.

"It's a mighty big room with plenty of places to sit and room to play," said Warner. "You can go have a look if you like."

The boy turned to look at Mary Ethel for approval.

Standing at the sink, wearing her day apron, she smiled, "Go ahead young fella. It's okay."

The boy did not move, but instead pointed at her apron and said, "Pink."

"Well, you can talk after all," she chuckled. "Yes, this apron is pink and it once belonged to my mother. Do you know any other colors?" she coaxed. He again stood silent and motionless. Mary Ethel looked at Warner and shrugged.

Finishing his coffee Warner asked, "You ready to get to town?"

"Just give me a minute," said Mary Ethel, "I want to finish these dishes and brush my hair."

Warner replied, "Alright, I'll be outside hitching up."

He walked off the back porch into the yard and noticed that the previous night's rain had not puddled. The ground was thirsty. It had been a good long while since it rained last.

He squatted low and picked up a handful of soil. He rubbed it between his fingers, testing for moisture. He thought about the winter wheat they had just sown into the fields. "*This rain will give that wheat a good chance to sprout before snow can fall,*" he thought.

Standing up, Warner wiped the soil on his britches leg and walked out to the horse barn. Opening the door, he could see Alice almost dancing in circles anticipating feeding time. He gave each horse hay and oats and tidied up around the paddock a bit before walking over to the elder of the two.

"Well, girls... we got a special mission for you today. I'll ask y'all to pull gentle and mind what I say," Warner said, "Now Molly, I need you to help me tame Alice." Molly turned back to her feed and Warner stroked her mane. He looked over at the other horse, who was busy with a can of oats, and whistled. Alice looked up from the feed can and shook her head up and down. Warner laughed, "Slow down girl. You eat that fast and your belly will swell up with gas... and we've got to ride behind you!"

Of the pair, Alice was always eager to team up and go to town. Molly had foaled her about three years back and nearly died in the process. The two of them were close, but Molly was beginning to show her age and slow a bit. Alice, on the other hand, had itchy feet. Often, Alice would get the better of her mother's nerves out in the pasture, by insisting on games and play, when all Molly wanted was to rest and graze off the tender tops of the new grass.

People aren't too different. Those among us who have more years behind, than in front, seem to be more interested in simple pleasures and a slower pace of life.

Warner and Mary Ethel were nearing that stage, but the previous day's events had called so much into question. Whatever lay ahead for them, one thing was sure; the future of the Malone family had now been tied to the fate of that little boy.

Warner stroked the blaze on Molly's face and gave her a pat on the cheek. "Good girl," he said and walked back to the house.

Chapter 4

Just Fine

The ride into town was no different from any other Warner and Mary Ethel had taken together during the nearly thirty years they had been married. Usually, the only time Warner hitched up the buckboard was for trips into town to purchase certain staples or sell crops. The buckboard was for hauling things that were either coming to or going from the Malone farm. Today Warner and Mary Ethel wondered which one it was for the boy.

Knowing their way to town, Molly and Alice had only to be coaxed into a preferred pace, too fast and the springs on the wagon seat couldn't keep up. When he was alone with "the girls" as he called them, Warner would often let them go a little faster. Mary Ethel however, preferred a smoother ride.

Warner held the reigns loosely with his wrists on his knees. He was singing a tune that made Mary Ethel smile. She began to sing along bouncing the boy in her lap.

"Ninety years without slumbering,

tick tock tick tock,

His life's seconds numbering,

tick tock tick tock,

it stopped, short,

never to go again when the old man died."

As the pair sang, the wagon rolled on and the hoof beats of the horses kept a steady rhythm. Warner loved to sing to pass the time. He sang in the choir at church when they needed him, but he got the most joy from singing with family and while he worked.

As Mary Ethel bounced the child, she looked at him smiling and asked, "Do you know this one little fella?" The child did not speak but almost cracked a smile. She pulled his head close and squeezed him tight. "Don't you worry son, the sheriff will have you back with your folks in no time."

"I expect this little one is going to be happy to get back with his people," she said, leaning down to look the boy in the face. Mary Ethel was expecting the child to smile, or in some other way express excitement and hope that he would soon be back with his family. Still, he was expressionless. She sat up and gave Warner a quizzical look.

Warner had an idea why the boy might not be eager to return to his kin, if the bruises he'd seen on him earlier were any indication of what his life back home was like. He didn't mention it to Mary Ethel, he knew it would hurt her heart to know, so he changed the subject and commented about the rain having stopped and the sun being out. She looked at Warner and studied his face and mannerisms closely. She could tell when he was keeping something from her. He'd never been able to surprise her completely. Once he'd given her a brand new store bought rocking chair for a surprise, but for weeks beforehand she knew he was up to something. When he was keeping a secret, Warner stopped talking as much as he normally did. A chatterbox at birth, he would become overly cautious that he might give away the secret he was keeping and so would clam up almost completely.

Mary Ethel could see all the same signs, he was holding something back, but she had no idea what it might be. She pulled her collar up around her ears and tucked the boy back inside her coat.

A few more miles, a few more songs, and they reached the sheriff's office.

Gordon Edwards was the duly elected Sheriff of Paige County. Paige was a quiet county inhabited by mostly peaceable folk. The need for a sheriff at all was slight compared to many other parts of the world. Still, Sheriff Edwards took pride in the fact that the good people in his county had trusted him with the job. He was firm but fair in the way he enforced the local ordinances and state laws in Paige County. He was a stickler for the Constitution and the rule of law, but he understood that while the one should never be compromised, the rules were sometimes flexible.

Pulling the wagon around the back of the building, Warner hopped off, tied the reigns to a post by the door, and then helped Mary Ethel down. Once again, the child had fallen asleep in her lap, and she was taking great care not to wake him.

"Give me a hand," she said, "this boy is as light as a feather, but I'm not as spry as I once was."

Warner took her hand and chuckled. "You were plenty spry the other week when we had the house to ourselves for two whole days."

Mary Ethel smacked his arm and blushed, "Hush your mouth husband or the whole town will hear you." He smiled and tried to steal a kiss but was rebuffed. Humming the wedding march, Warner held the door for Mary Ethel as she carried the child into the sheriff's office.

Walking past Warner, she gave him *that look* meaning play-time was over. "Yes Ma'am," said Warner.

"Well, good morning Malones," called out the sheriff. "What brings you into town?" He was about to ask the obvious question, when Mary Ethel began...

"Warner and Edward found him last night wandering up the road from town all by himself. He wasn't too far from the whistle stop at Wayside," she said. Rubbing the sleeping boy's back, she added, "And he was near about froze to death."

As she entered the room, Warner pulled a chair around for her to sit next to the pot-bellied stove. Mary Ethel took her seat, careful not to jostle the boy awake; she positioned the child near the stove to warm him.

"Do you have any idea who he belongs to?" asked the sheriff.

"No idea at all Gordy. I don't recognize him and he doesn't favor anyone we know. He looks to be about 4 years old to me," said Warner.

"What's the boy's name?" asked the sheriff.

Mary Ethel, shaking her head, replied, "We have no idea. He hasn't spoken a word since we found him...except for one."

Gordy looked worried but intrigued at the same time. "What one word was that?" he asked.

"Pink," she answered.

"Just that one word is all we've heard him say so far," added Warner.

Sheriff Edwards leaned against the corner of his desk and crossed his arms. He took a deep breath, let out a sigh, and then scratched the back of his head. He'd dealt with all the customary trouble a small town would typically have. Once in a while, he had to settle a business quarrel, or offer to let Beauregard Harris sleep it off on a cot in the jail when his wife Dorothy had run him out of the house for being drunk—but he'd never had a lost child on his hands.

"Well, I reckon I can call over to Charlottesville and maybe to Richmond, and see if there's a bulletin out for a missing boy," said Gordy.

Warner could see that the boy was awake but pretending to be asleep. He caught the child's eye, but the boy instantly shut it and pretended to be sleeping. He wondered about the bruises, and whether the boy even wanted to go home. Whatever the case, the little lost child did not belong to them and had to be returned to his family.

Smiling and shaking his head Warner asked, "And I suppose you'd like us to see to the boy while you look for his folks?" He glanced at Mary Ethel, who was already nodding her head in agreement.

"Well, I figure that would be best. Do you agree Mary Ethel?" asked the sheriff.

She looked right at Warner and said, "I certainly do."

Warner laughed and said, "Well, looks like we're gonna have company for a few days. Don't worry about the boy Gordy, he'll be in good hands at the Malone place."

Mary Ethel stood up with the child still feigning sleep and started toward the door.

"Uh, Sheriff, I wonder if I might have a word with you about your re-election campaign?" asked Warner as he gestured toward the back room.

Mary Ethel looked puzzled but shrugged it off.

"Wait here darling, I'll only be a minute," said Warner.

Gordy and Warner stepped just into the back of the Sheriff's office where the two jail cells were.

"Warner you know I'm not up for re-election for another two and a half years! What's this about now?" asked the sheriff.

Warner leaned against the doorpost and said, "Gordy, the boy's been beaten."

"Beaten?" asked the Sheriff. "How do you know?" His tone carried surprise and heartbreak.

Nodding to show his shared concern, Warner replied, "This morning I took him to the outhouse to relieve himself and when I helped him with his britches I saw a good many bruises all over."

"Have mercy!" said the sheriff. "Can you have Doc Webber give him a lookin' over? I expect he's probably up and around by now."

"Mary Ethel was already figurin' to have Dr. Webber

examine the boy, but she doesn't know about the bruises. I haven't told her because I just know it'll hurt her heart," answered Warner.

"Well, she'll find out soon enough. But look," said the sheriff, "if you want, I can go fetch the doctor on my automobile so you won't have to ride out to his place."

Warner gave a relieved sigh, reached out, and shook Gordy's hand. "That's mighty nice of you sheriff," he said.

Motioning for Warner to join him in the main office, Gordy replied, "My pleasure."

In the office, Mary Ethel had sat back down in the chair and was trying to coax a conversation out of the boy, who had given up feigning sleep. Sheriff Edwards noticed that his hair was a tangled mess, and that he had no socks.

"I'll wager Mr. Harold would be happy to cut the boy's hair at no charge," offered the sheriff. "I expect he'll feel a lot better once he's good and cleaned up," he added.

"Well," said Warner, "Why don't we walk him across the street to Mr. Harold's barbershop and get him a haircut while we wait for you to come back with the Doc."

Mary Ethel thought it was a fine idea to get the child's hair trimmed. Running her hand over his head, she commented on how soft and fine it was. "Many a poor girl has surely sat brushing her hair wishing for as fine a-locks as these," she said.

She and Warner carried the boy over to the barbershop, and when they stepped through the door Anthony Harold greeted them the way he greeted everyone.

"Haircuts ten cents, shaves are a nickel, and gossip is free."

"Good morning Tony," said Warner.

Mary Ethel came in through the door carrying the boy and when Tony saw him, he looked surprised and asked, "Well, who's that you got there?"

"Well," said Mary Ethel, "This little fella is lost and we're gonna mind him while the sheriff finds his folks."

Tony spun the barber chair around and removed a pair of boots he'd been shining when they came in. He put the booster seat across the arms of the chair and gave the seat a pat. "Climb up here and have a seat, young fella, and we'll get that mop shaped up lickety-split."

Mary Ethel put the boy on the chair and he sat there without moving or speaking. Mr. Harold made an attempt at small talk, but the child said nothing.

"He's a quiet little thing isn't he?" remarked the barber.

Warner and Mary Ethel agreed and went on to tell Mr. Harold the entire story. They asked if he knew who he might belong to; being as barbers, sheriffs, and tax collectors usually knew everyone around.

Tony walked over in front of the boy to finish up and said, "I don't reckon I have any idea who he might belong to. He's a well-mannered boy, if you get lucky you might get to keep him."

Along about the time Warner was offering to pay Mr. Harold for the haircut, and he was refusing to take their money, Sheriff Edwards walked in with Doc Webber.

"Mornin' Sheriff, mornin' Doc," said Tony.

Doctor Webber explained that he was there to examine the boy, and since the shop was empty of anyone else, he offered to examine him there. Tony, Warner, and Sheriff Edwards excused themselves and went out the back. Mr. Harold had some home-made wine that he'd bottled the week before, and he was eager to have Gordy and Warner's opinion.

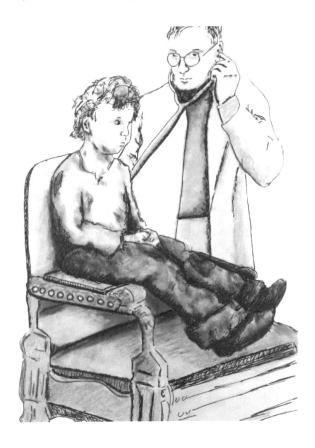

Doc Webber examined the boy while he sat perfectly still on the booster chair. He listened to him breathing and then to his heartbeat. He looked in his ears, down his throat, and into his eyes.

He looked at Mary Ethel with a concerned expression. She suspected he'd heard the thing in his chest she'd felt the previous night. Doctor Webber placed his stethoscope against the boy's chest once again. He listened longer this time until the child became restless.

"Hold still young man," he said.

After the doctor was satisfied with the first part of the examination, he said, "Well, that will suffice for your top half. Now, let's take down your trousers and examine the rest of you."

Mary Ethel moved the checkerboard off of a side table. She picked up the boy and stood him on it, so the Doc could do a thorough examination.

When Doctor Webber slipped the boys britches down, he recoiled at the sight of so many bruises. Mary Ethel put her hand over her mouth and gasped, "Dear Lord Almighty!"

Doc Webber looked at Mary Ethel and shook his head. "This is not good. Not good at all."

After he'd examined the little fellow, he set him down on the floor. Doc Webber took off his stethoscope and headlamp, and packed them back in his bag. He fidgeted with the bag for a moment. He was stalling, thinking of how to tell Mary Ethel what he'd heard inside the boy's chest. Deciding the direct approach was best, he simply blurted it out.

"He has a heart murmur," explained the doc. "It's possible he will grow out of it and that the heart will repair itself over time, but it's impossible to know. He really needs to go see a specialist. His family will need to be informed, so the condition can be monitored," explained Dr. Webber.

He paused and then addressed the other issue, "And these bruises can only mean one thing."

Mary Ethel struggled to make sense of how anyone could beat a child. Doc Webber, noticing the confused and shocked expression on her face, nodded in agreement.

He then excused himself out the back to tell Sheriff Edwards what he'd seen. He too was eager to taste the wine he'd heard rumor of earlier.

Mary Ethel helped the child dress, and unable to stop herself, hugged him tight. Her heart was aching for him, and suddenly she felt as motherly toward him as she'd ever felt toward any of her own brood.

She rocked him in her arms and whispered, "You're gonna be just fine, little fella. You're gonna be just fine."

Chapter 5

Dirt-N-All

No life is free from ups and downs, bumps and bruises, good times and bad. Every person's experience is unique, and some are even fortunate enough to have a fairly smooth ride in the early years of life. A good home, loving parents, and the freedom to become their own distinct person, serve as a recipe for a fine, enjoyable childhood.

However, there are some, like this little lost boy, whose past may not seem as neat and clean; whose past is both messy and dirty. It takes a special heart to look beyond the chaos and dirt, and see the beauty and goodness beneath. Leola Joann Malone had just such a heart.

When Warner and Mary Ethel returned home from the sheriff's office with the boy, Victoria seemed to be the most excited. Having agreed to care for the child while the sheriff tried to locate his family, Warner and Mary Ethel rearranged a spare bedroom to suit him. Vicky and Mary Ethel went to work making up the bed, placing a chamber pot in the room, and dusting off the chest-of-drawers.

"This poor child hasn't a single decent thread to wear," said Mary Ethel, "Let's go up in the attic and see if we can find some of Ed'ard and CD's old things that might fit him."

She and Vicky spent a good hour going through several old trunks filled with clothes that had long since become too small for any of the Malone children. When they emerged from the attic, they were confident that they'd collected a suitable wardrobe for the little guy. Mary Ethel and Vicky took care to wash the clothes, fold them neatly, and place them in drawers.

For several weeks, Sheriff Edwards sent telegrams, wrote letters, and made telephone calls to agencies all across the Commonwealth of Virginia trying to find out anything about the boy.

In response to an inquiry from the sheriff, a representative from the state adoption agency came to visit the child, and unable to make him talk, determined that he must be simple and in need of special care. The bureaucrat informed Sheriff Edwards that if no parents were located, and no one was willing to take him in, he would need to go to an orphanage in Richmond for children with disabilities.

Over the weeks the authorities were searching for his parents, the Malones housed and fed the boy, while Vicky kept him entertained. She took him for walks, and let him play with a wooden ball that had once adorned a post on an old bed. She read to him, sang to him, and generally mothered him.

Despite the love and care he received, the child did not speak, and he only allowed Mary Ethel to hold him. The little fellow even refused to eat unless comfortably seated in her lap. His behavior perplexed the Malone family, but it honored Mary Ethel to be the child's favorite place of refuge. Perhaps it was her soothing voice, her gentle touch, or her words of encouragement and hopefulness that attracted the boy, but in any case, it warmed her heart, whenever he climbed into her lap.

The Malones decided to call him Pink, until they discovered his real name. He seemed to be agreeable; as he responded each time it was called.

Many times the boy left his bed in the night and climbed into Warner and Mary Ethel's. On a few occasions he awakened them in fits, tossing and turning and even crying out in his sleep. When asked, Doc Webber explained that the night terrors were likely due to the awful abuse he had endured.

Day after day, they waited for news about the boy's family but none came. By and by, it became Mary Ethel's prayer, that if he had no family of his own, they would be granted guardianship of the little fellow. She even convinced Warner to let the sheriff know that they would give the boy a home, if needed.

They had even discussed the matter with their son CD and his wife, Leola. They'd been married for about seven years and were unable to have any children of their own. The sheriff agreed that CD and Leola would be a fine choice for the little boy. As for Leola, she was as excited as any person might be. However, she tried not to think about the prospect of adopting Pink too much. She'd suffered two miscarriages previously and dared not risk another heartbreak. Disappointment had taught her to fear the hope, of ever becoming a mother.

Warner, too, fretted over what he saw happening. He could see, plain as day that Mary Ethel, and the whole family for that matter, had begun to develop deep feelings for the boy. He knew it would break a great many tender hearts when it was time for Pink to return to his own family.

On a Friday evening, about two weeks before Christmas, Warner was outside buttoning up the livestock for the night, when he saw the dim glow of headlamps coming up the dirt road toward their farm. He finished closing up the barn, waited on the porch, and listened as the automobile approached.

As it neared the house, Warner could make out the letters on the door of the car, "Paige Co. Sheriff's Office." He braced himself and tried to think of what to say to help Mary Ethel accept the inevitable. It seemed to Warner that the only reason the sheriff would ride his automobile all the way out to their place, so late in the evening, was to fetch the boy and return him to his family.

Gordy pulled around behind the house and shut off the automobile. It sputtered a bit and backfired as the engine stopped. To his consternation, the loud bang drew everyone out of the house, and Warner knew there wasn't going to be an easy way for the family to hear the news. They would just have to hear it, straight from the sheriff's mouth.

Gordy stepped out and shut the door. He walked around the

front of the car, over to the porch where Warner was standing and shook his hand.

"Evening, Warner," he said.

"Good evening Sheriff. What brings you all the way out here so late?" questioned Warner.

Sheriff Edwards turned to Mary Ethel, Vicky, and Edward, who were standing on the porch in a bunch, almost as if they were waiting for a photograph. Mary Ethel was holding the boy, and the sheriff made an effort to greet him specifically.

"This is about the boy, isn't it?" asked Mary Ethel.

There was a tremor in her voice. She had dreaded this moment and did not notice that her embrace of the boy had instinctively gotten tighter and tighter until the child grunted and pushed away. Putting the boy down on the porch, Mary Ethel patted him on the head and apologized.

"Yes, it's about the boy," he answered.

He squatted down in front of the porch where the child was standing and said, "Well, little fella, we have called everyone we know to call, we've written letters, sent telegrams, and even put a notice in two of the biggest newspapers east of the Blue Ridge, but we haven't been able to locate your family."

Mary Ethel put her hands over her mouth and gave a hopeful gasp. Her heart leapt at what she hoped Gordy would say next.

"Seeing as we haven't been able to find your family, you will be staying with the Malones from now on, unless your folks show up to claim you."

The Sheriff stood up, and looking at Warner asked, "If that's still alright?"

Warner opened his mouth to answer, but Mary Ethel beat him to the draw.

"Yes, yes, yes, indeed it will be just fine, we will gladly take the boy," she gushed.

Laughing Warner replied, "Well, I was gonna say it would be fine too."

"Well, then I guess it's settled. I'll file the papers the state agent left for me in the event we found him a home," said Gordy. "You'll need to come in to the office and sign everything in front of witnesses, and then we just wait for the adoption papers to come back through the mail."

"Is that all we have to do?" asked Warner.

The sheriff assured them that there would likely be a visit or two from a state agent sometime in the future, but for the most part, it was a sure bet the matter was settled.

The following morning, Warner rode out to CD and Leola's place and informed them that Sheriff Edwards had been unable to find out anything about Pink's family.

Sitting at the kitchen table with his son and daughter-in-law, Warner thought carefully about what to say, and how to say it. His heart was torn about the matter. On the one hand, he was saddened that the boy's family could not be located, but on the other, he wasn't sure that it was a bad thing—judging by the bruises they'd found on his little body.

"Dad, do you want a cup of coffee?" asked CD.

Warner sat down and smiling replied, "Indeed, I would."

CD poured the coffee, while Leola set a fresh batch of breakfast muffins on the table. She was antsy to hear the news. Leola was sure that Warner had dropped by to fill them in on the status of the little boy.

She wanted to give him a home and become a mother so badly that she dared not even think of it. Leola had wrestled with the whole matter for weeks, since Mary Ethel had first suggested that she and CD might be able to give the child a home.

She didn't want to steal the boy or keep him from his family, but from what she knew about the abuse the boy had suffered; it gave her peace that maybe they would be rescuing him.

"Well," began Warner sipping his coffee, "Gordy came out to our place last night and told us that he hasn't heard anything about the boy's folks, and if you're willing, the Commonwealth gives him discretion about who should take him in."

Playing coy, Warner picked up his cup and took another sip. CD and Leola were bright people and knew that this must mean they would be given charge of Pink, but they needed to hear it spoken.

"So...," demanded CD.

Grinning as wide as the Shenandoah, Warner replied, "If you'll have him, the boy is yours to raise."

Leola leapt from her chair, threw her arms around Warner's neck, and kissed his cheek. CD stood up and hugged Leola. He lifted her off the ground and twirled her around in the air. When he set her down on the floor, he kissed her forehead and said, "Congratulations mama."

"Alright you two," said Warner, "I reckon I'll go home and

fetch the boy out here to you. Mary Ethel will want to come along."

"Daddy, we could go get him. It's no trouble," replied CD

Warner smiled at Leola. He knew that she was eager to begin nesting. "Best you stay here and help your wife see to his accommodations."

CD agreed, and he and Leola got to work making up the bed in the room that would no longer be considered "the spare."

When Warner arrived home, he told Mary Ethel how thrilled CD and Leola were to take the child in. She hadn't the slightest doubt that they would give Pink a home, and she already had his things packed. He didn't have much more than a few changes of clothes and an old jacket that all of the children had worn at some stage in their lives.

"Where is the boy?" asked Warner.

"Outside with Vicky, somewhere," she answered.

When it was time to leave, Mary Ethel began calling out from the back porch for Victoria and Pink to come into the house. After a few minutes, they emerged from the hayloft. Pink and Vicky were covered in hay dust, dirt, and grins. They'd been swinging on a rope that Joe had hung up in the rafters years ago when he was a boy. There was a wooden plank at the bottom for a seat, and what a fine swing it made.

Vicky poked her head out of the loft door and answered her mother, "Yes ma'am?"

"Get yourselves down here at once!" shouted Mary Ethel. She was a bit put out that the pair were so dirty, but in any case, it was time to leave.

"I'm sorry!" shouted the boy.

Vicky was astonished. These were the first words she'd hear him speak. "Don't you worry none," she assured, "Let's go see what mama wants."

Climbing onto the wagon the four of them travelled the four and a half miles out to CD and Leola's farm. All along the way, the Malones talked and sang. The mood was light and joyful. Mary Ethel had explained to Pink that he was going to be staying with CD and Leola. The boy made no reply, but neither did he protest.

Vicky was busy in the back of the wagon playing with Pink. They were rolling the wooden ball back and forth as the wagon rattled along. The bumps and jostles made the game much more entertaining and challenging. The sound of their laughter made Mary Ethel smile. She reached a hand over and patted her husband's back.

"You're a good man, Warner Malone," she said.

He smiled and nodded his head, "We're good people."

Warner thought back to the night he and Edward had found the boy. He remembered the prayers he'd prayed, for wisdom and goodness. It was clear to him that the Lord was being generous to them. There was goodness afoot and it made him glad.

From the back of the wagon, Vicky called out, "Mama, does this all mean that I get to be 'Aunt Vicky'?"

Mary Ethel turned in her seat to face her and answered, "I guess so, sweetheart."

This made Vicky quite happy. She produced a smile so infectious that it spread across the wagon to Pink's little face.

Early on, as the family anticipated the possibility that they would adopt him, CD and Leola spent a fair amount of time with him. At church and then during Sunday dinners, they had taken the time to play with and talk to him. Though silent most of the time, Pink seemed to warm up to Leola. Once, while she was reading to Pink, out on the front porch, he got out of his chair, climbed into her lap, and eventually fell asleep.

Pulling into the yard at CD's place, Warner hollered out announcing their arrival. CD and Leola came out on the back porch and waited for everyone to climb down.

Vicky led the boy by the hand as they, all four, approached the house. Vicky stopped just short of the steps and squatted in front of Pink. She reached down to wipe the dirt off of his face, but he protested and pulled away. Vicky mussed his hair and said, "Well, little man, you're home."

Home, home was a word Pink did not know. He'd heard the word, but it held no meaning. Inside his fragile little soul, he'd heard whispers, rumors of acceptance, and unencumbered joy but had never felt it. He had never known anything except over-crowded orphanages and smelly boxcars. More than that, he had never known love. He'd never known security, safety, or lack of want. All of that was destined to change. In the span of just a month, he had gone from being an abused captive, to being placed in one of the most loving families in the county.

Vicky stood up and faced CD and Leola as if she herself was presenting them with their son.

"I reckon he's all yours," she laughed.

CD smiled back and chided, "Hmmm, I guess he'll clean up alright."

Leola stepped down off the porch and marched over in front of the boy. She knelt in the dirt in front of him and put her hands on his shoulders. Her teary eyes now glistening in the sunlight, she exclaimed, with indignation, "Clean up? Why, he's perfect... dirt-n-all."

Dirt and all. Those words rang like liberty in Pink's heart. His new mother's affirmation produced a smile. He was too young to understand what it all meant, but he could sure feel it. He felt loved. He felt safe. He felt good all over, and for the first time he was beginning to feel like he belonged somewhere.

"Dirt-n-all." were the only details he would remember about that day. And for the rest of his life, it was the way Pink described anything he thought was perfect. The phrase even became part of the Malone family lexicon. All because Leola saw his value, his potential, and his goodness... *dirt-n-all.*

Chapter 6

All Abuzz About Rain

In the four years since Warner and Edward had found Pink, he gradually began to accept that the Malones were his family now. He grew to love CD and Leola and truly thought of them as his mom and dad. He loved Mary Ethel too, but the connection he had with Warner was unearthly. A mystical union seemed to be on full display whenever they were together. Whenever Pink had serious trouble or heartache, Warner was the one who was asked to help.

He would often take Pink fishing, or on buggy rides to talk about his mischief or his fears. Pink had a sophisticated sense of humor and a vivid imagination, so mischief came easily for him. More often than not, the family said little about Pink's pranks and shenanigans. They all figured he'd grow out of it soon enough.

The night terrors worried CD and Leola the most. For the first year after they'd adopted him, Pink had a bad dream almost every night. They say time heals all wounds. That may be true for some, or even most, but not for Pink. Time may have successfully covered over the trauma of his early childhood, but the scars made trusting anyone nearly impossible. In the event of any trouble or mischief he'd caused there was somewhere a whisper, "You don't belong here."

Many times Pink acted out, screaming and crying at CD and Leola. His little damaged heart, along with fear made him wary of believing anyone who claimed to love him. Pastor Donnie Briscoe once told CD that he thought the boy was putting them to the test; giving them a chance to prove they loved him—without condition.

In time, things seemed to settle into a comfortable rhythm.

The summer of 1918 was a particularly difficult time for the Malones and most other folks in Paige County. In fact, that year was especially hard for many around the world as *The Great War* was raging along the Western Front. No one in Paige County had ever heard of the many towns and villages described in the newspapers, save Paris.

Although, newspaper articles tried to describe the "normal" horrors of war along with all the hellish conditions associated with trench warfare, the awful day-to-day living conditions were unimaginable. Man's inhumanity toward man makes it impossible for folks back home to empathize, unless they have experienced such atrocities firsthand.

No one in the Malone family, who was still living, had been to war. Warner's daddy had been conscripted into the Confederate Army in 1863, but when he came home from the war, he seldom spoke of his experiences. And it had been quite a few years now, since he passed away. It's interesting that when the old folks talked about war, they never glamourized it or made it out to be more than the nightmare that it is.

Edward James Malone was the youngest of Warner and Mary Ethel's children. He was the boy in the family who was always up for an adventure. His mother called him a "thrill-seeker". She was right as rain about Edward, or Ed'ard as most people called him. When he was only twelve years old, he jumped from an eighty-foot cliff into Turtle Lake. Everyone knew him as a daredevil, so no one was surprised when he enlisted in the United States Army at the age of 18. The "War to End All Wars", which was already being hotly contested in France, called to his sense of adventure. In the summer of 1917, Ed'ard went to Camp Lee for his basic training. The day he took the train out of Luray was the last time the family had seen him. Thankfully, Ed'ard was quite good about writing during his time at Camp Lee. He would send a letter home most weeks and describe the many different boys he'd met from all over Virginia and some from other states too. Everyone was praying for the boys "over there" and in the Malone family, it was no exception.

They spent most Sunday afternoons with all the children and grandchildren gathered for Sunday dinner at Warner and Mary Ethel's house. The mood was always light and joyful. Stories, singalongs, and games were the norm. There was no shortage of life in their family, but all that changed when Ed'ard left Camp Lee for Europe.

His regular weekly letters stopped and the Malones no longer felt as connected to him. Often Mary Ethel would sit out on the front porch, rock in her chair, and pray in silence for her baby boy.

To make matters worse, the summer of 1918 was exceptionally dry in Paige Valley. There hadn't been any rain in six weeks or more. Corn, cotton, and tobacco crops were looking mighty poor. It was so bad that Pastor Donnie Briscoe had called a meeting at the church every morning at 9 o'clock, so folks could pray for rain.

"If we don't get rain in the next week or two, I'm afraid we'll lose every stalk of corn we've planted," said Warner.

Warner's brother Jim, sitting on the edge of the porch, shook his head and replied, "I ain't seen it this bad since I was a boy. I recall, one year when you were a baby, we had a drought that lasted all summer. There wasn't a single thing to harvest. Fact is, we had to water the vegetable plants from the well, or we would've starved, I reckon."

Warner nodded his head in agreement. "I'm watering my garden from the well now," he replied.

Jim rubbed the back of his neck, took off his hat, and wiped the sweat from his brow. "The rest of the folks around are doing the same, I expect," he added.

It wasn't at all unusual for folks to gather to pray during times of need, and this sure was one of those times.

"Well, I reckon I'll be going to the prayer meetin' tomorrow. Will I see you there?" asked Jim.

Warner shook his head, "No, I've promised CD I would help him side his new barn this week. We're taking Molly and Alice to fetch a load of board and batten from the planing mill, first thing in the morning."

"Alright then, I'll say a prayer for Ed'ard tomorrow too," replied Jim. "Any word yet?"

Warner stood up from the edge of the porch. He grimaced and stretching his back, answered, "No, not a word so far. He's only been shipped out a couple of months, but no, nothing yet. Mary Ethel is awfully tore up about it all. Some nights she can't sleep and just sits up all night, on the front porch, rockin' in that chair of hers."

"I never heard of such," said Jim, "so many countries, at war, all at once."

Warner wanted to change the subject. He worried and fretted about Edward as much as anyone but made a great effort not to show it around others. He simply prayed that the good Lord would keep him safe. Most of the time, he tried not to think about it too much.

"Well, let me go. I've got a few chores to do before it gets dark on me," said Warner. He climbed up on the buckboard wagon and gave Molly a signal to get moving.

The following morning at CD and Leola's place, the day had begun around the usual time. CD had been up since about 6 a.m. feeding the chickens and milking Gerty. When he came back in the house for breakfast, Leola was up and had already made a stack of breakfast muffins, fried potatoes and onions, and had a good, hot pot of coffee on the boil.

"Charles, what time is your daddy going to be here? she

asked. "I've made plenty for him to eat with us, if he hasn't already."

"I don't know exactly when he'll get here, but I imagine he's eaten already," replied CD.

Leola and CD sat together at the table, said a blessing, and ate their breakfast. After a while, Pink came into the kitchen rubbing his eyes.

"You're up early," said his mother. "Were we making too much noise for you to sleep?"

"No ma'am," he replied, "I didn't want to miss Grandpa when he comes over."

Pink, still half asleep, stumbled over and climbed into Leola's lap. He reached for her plate, but she brushed his hand away.

"Young man, I will thank you to ask before you put your hand in my plate," said Leola with an incredulous smile on her face.

Pink smiled back and replied, "Sorry mama. May I have a muffin please?"

"You may indeed," said Leola.

CD chuckled. He was proud of the way Leola was with Pink. She was gentle and loving toward the boy but never compromised good manners and couth.

As Leola went about finishing her breakfast, Pink sat in her lap and did his best to help. At one point, CD got up and fetched another stack of muffins from inside the stove to refill her plate.

A half-hour passed, Pink helped his mama with the dishes,

and CD got a couple of small chores done while they waited for Warner to arrive.

Pink waited by the window and watched for Molly and Alice pulling the buckboard. When Warner climbed down off the wagon, Pink was already in the yard.

"Granddaddy!" he exclaimed, "look what I can do."

Pink pulled his peashooter from his hip pocket, placed a special smooth stone in its pouch, and fired it at a coffee can he'd set up on the fence by the mule barn.

Warner grinned and watched as the stone arched upward and then down.

"Ting!" the stone knocked the can off the fence with a satisfying report.

"Attaboy!" hollered Warner, "I expect you to have me a rabbit or a squirrel to eat next time I come by."

"I can go find you one right now Granddaddy," said Pink.

CD walked over from the well house with a couple of ten-quart pails of water for Molly and Alice and set them down in front of the two horses. "Son, your granddaddy and I don't have time to skin a rabbit right now, we've got to head into Lurray to pick up my order from the lumber mill," explained CD.

Pink smiled and asked if he could come along, but CD reminded him that he'd promised to accompany his mother to the church that morning for the prayer meeting.

When they pulled out for town, Pink raced alongside the wagon until they got out to the road. Walking back to the house, he took a shortcut through the pecan grove and jumped a rabbit.

"That would've made a good supper," he thought.

By the time he finally meandered back into the house, it was a little past seven o'clock.

His mother was ready and had made a sack lunch for the two of them.

"Do your mother a favor and tote this basket please," said Leola.

"Yes ma'am," came the boy's reply. "Mama, can I stay outside and play with the other kids today? It's too stuffy inside the church, and the preacher takes too long."

"Mind your manners—and yes, you may," she replied.

Pink thanked his mother and gave her a grateful hug. The prayer meeting was sure to be an hour or two or even longer depending on how much *in earnest* Pastor Donnie decided to get that day.

Soon, Leola and Pink started off to the church. All along the way, Pink wandered to and fro, back and forth, and this way and that.

He found butterflies, toads, and a pocket full of perfectly smooth rocks that Pink said were, "just the right size" for his peashooter.

"If you put one more rock in your britches pockets, your belt is gonna give up, and everyone at the church is gonna see you in your skivvies," said his mother.

Pink smiled and patted his right pocket. "I got enough rocks to start a war."

"Hush child," cautioned Leola, "you know nothing about war, and I pray you never do."

The pair walked the rest of the way in relative silence. Pink knew that his mother was worried about his Uncle Ed'ard being "gone off to war", but he didn't really understand where his uncle was or where *war* even was. So, when he asked his grandmother a few weeks ago, where Edward was, she really didn't know exactly, so she just told Pink, "he's somewhere in God's world."

As simple as the answer sounds, it made the whole concept of war and distance seem small and manageable for his young mind and especially for his tender little heart.

When they reached the church Leola went inside and helped get the windows raised before the sanctuary became too warm.

Outside, Pink found his cousins Elijah and Jim, and a few of the other boys. They had already set up a row of rocks on a fence and were doing their best to knock them off with their peashooters. Some of the girls were outside playing games too, but according to Jim, had already made it very plain that the boys were not invited, on account of them being "smelly."

Pink usually didn't mind. He was uninterested in the girls. Most of them never liked to have any fun—at least not the kind of fun Pink liked to have. They never seemed to appreciate the skill required to catch a bullfrog, or climb up and pick the highest apple in the tree. Girls were "boring and fancy" according to Pink.

But on this day, there was a new girl at the church. She was playing with the other girls near the entrance to the building. Pink had never seen her before, and she was remarkable. She had long blonde hair that hung in curls past her shoulders, a bright smile, and a bouncy confident air about her.

Pink was mesmerized. He stood staring at the girl for the longest time until she noticed him and waved. Pink blushed and ran back over to where the boys were playing.

"C'mon," said Jim. "Let's see who can knock a rock off the fence from the farthest away."

Jim Hawkins was the oldest of all the cousins in their family and was bigger, by far, than Pink. Pink looked up to Jim and sometimes that got him trouble because he was always out to impress him.

For a solid hour, a dozen boys passed the time firing rocks from their peashooters at anything and everything—until Jim happened to look over and see something extraordinary.

A hive of bees had swarmed and was looking for a new home. When honeybees swarm it is because the colony has outgrown its present location, and having produced more queens, it is ready to divide up and plant a new colony else- where. While the hive is deciding on which queen should call the shots, they swarm together in a giant ball— a large mass of bees all crawling around on top of one another— usually in a treetop or in a bush.

Today, however, this swarm of bees had collected them- selves under the eaves of the church. It was a magnificent sight to behold. There must have been ten thousand bees clinging to the edge of the roof. Some of the bees were still flying around trying to find a space to land in the swarm, but most had already found a spot. The mass of bees quivered and moved in place like a single giant organism.

The boys were admiring the buzzing, ball of bees that hovered at least forty feet away, when out of the blue, Jim turned to Pink and said, "I bet you can't hit that swarm of bees with your peashooter?"

Pink was offended. He looked hurt. Everything about Pink, his manhood, his skills as a hunter, a warrior, and all the other noble things an eight-year-old boy thinks himself to be, had been called into question.

Pink reached in his pocket and felt for a smooth stone. He was after the perfect rock he'd found earlier. "You hide and watch!" exclaimed a defiant Pink.

He put the stone in the leather pouch of the peashooter and stretched the inner tube back as far as his little arm was able. He let the stone fly and like lightning, it flew straight and true smashing into the swarm of bees near the bottom.

Jim was astonished but tried not to show it. "Betcha can't do it again," he quipped.

Without a word, Pink produced another stone, this time much larger, and with the same deadly aim as before, he let it loose.

He had to aim up a little more (to account for the increased weight of the larger stone) so when it came crashing down into the swarm, it knocked about half the bees off—— *and into an open church window.*

Frozen in fear, none of the boys moved—not even to blink. Pink was scared so spitless his tongue stuck to the roof of his mouth. No one could believe what had just happened, but reality set in the moment they heard dozens of screeching screams coming from inside the sanctuary.

In a split second, men and women began pouring out of the church swatting the air like escapees from an insane asylum.

Mrs. Clara was the Deacon Willie Duncan's wife of forty years. She was quite a large woman and in her panic, she cleared the door of the church bowling over three other members who were too busy swatting at bees to see her coming.

When she fell off the porch onto the ground, she flipped head over heels and landed with her dress over her face, revealing the brightest red bloomers anyone had ever seen. Several ladies rushed over to help her get up off the ground and recover her decency.

Inside, Pastor Donnie had shown courage and calm assisting the members out of the church, but as a great many angry bees found their way under his preaching robe, he instantly transformed from a calm, rational shepherd into an insane madman. He jumped and wailed and threw off his robe as quickly as he could, all the while forgetting that, due to the excessive heat, he'd elected to wear only his boxer shorts underneath.

All of the members stood outside, and through the opened doors of the church, watched their preacher inside the sanctuary dancing, flailing his arms, and shouting in his under-britches and gartered socks. Realizing what he'd done, he came to himself and ran out of the back of the sanctuary to the fellowship hall.

Leola burst from the door of the church and shouted one word... "Pink!"

When the bees invaded the church, she knew Pink had to have been involved. She stopped at the bottom of the steps in front of the church and spun in a circle, searching the yard for her son.

As soon as she made eye contact with Pink, he broke into a sprint, but his little legs were no match for Leola's. Running at an angle, she easily cut him off. In only a few strides she caught up and grabbed the collar of his shirt. Pink's feet flew up in the air and he landed on his back in the grass.

As soon as he hit the ground, she scooped him up in her arms and marched him home. When they were out of sight of the church, Leola put him down and said, "Not a word young man." The walk back home was as quiet as the prayer service had been, until the bees that is.

As Leola and Pink walked up the path into the yard, CD and Warner could be heard singing and hammering nails. Pink swallowed hard. He knew he was in a heap of trouble but neither his mother nor his father had ever spanked him. He took comfort in that fact, but still, he'd never emptied a prayer meeting with a swarm of bees before.

CD looked down from the ladder he was standing on and waved at Leola.

"Must have been a short meeting," said Warner.

Immediately, CD could see something was wrong.

He climbed down, took off his nail apron, and motioned to his father. Leola had Pink by the hand as they walked toward the new barn where the men were working. CD and Warner walked over to the water bucket under a sycamore tree and took a drink.

Warner gave CD a sly but worried look, "the boy's done something."

"I b'lieve you're right. Must have been a whopper," replied CD

When they got over to the shade of the sycamore tree, Leola gave Pink a gentle nudge in the back and said, "Now explain yourself to your daddy!"

Pink was already crying. Tears streamed down his little mischievous cheeks as he stared at his feet. Mumbling, sniffling, and stammering Pink retold the story as best he could remember it.

Every... horrifying... detail.

When he explained that Jim had challenged his abilities with the peashooter, Warner nodded his head in understanding. But CD was visibly angry, and when Pink told the part about the pastor stripping down to his underwear in the sanctuary, he interrupted Pink and sent him in the house.

"You go to your room. I want you to pray at least thirty minutes and tell the Lord you're sorry."

"Yes sir," replied Pink as he sulked his way to the house.

"We'll never be able to show our face at that church again, as long as we live!" exclaimed an exasperated Leola.

CD gave her a hug and kissed her forehead, "I hope it's not quite that bad darling."

Warner spoke up and assured her that Donnie Briscoe was a reasonable man who would likely come to see some sort of humor in the whole event, given enough time.

Warner sat down on a large stone under the tree and asked, "Do you two mind if I take the boy for a little walk to talk to him about it?"

Leola nodded in agreement. She looked at CD and said, "I think that is a wonderful idea. Right now, I'm so mad at him...I could chew nails!"

CD suppressed a grin. He could picture the preacher dancing in the sanctuary in nothing but his under-britches.

"Let's finish up. We're at a good stopping point. After dinner, I'll take him for a walk or maybe we'll ride out to Jim's and talk it over while we hunt up supper at the fishpond," suggested Warner.

"I suppose that'll be fine," replied CD

Chapter 7

Love's Kind

Life's experiences sometimes blend moments of triumph and loss in ways that, especially when we are young, become indistinguishable. And in our youth, as is so often the case, events run together in such a way that good mixes with bad so thoroughly that it creates a third thing altogether.

When Mary Ethel's mother passed away, she did so peacefully in her sleep. Hers was a death most would envy. She was not sick, she wasn't in any pain, and she was already living on borrowed time. However, she died on Mary Ethel's birthday. Ever since then, she hadn't cared to celebrate it because her birthday carried with it the tragic memory of losing her mother.

A beautiful summer day filled with family and laughter, which ends in tragedy, may color our emotions about sunny summer days for the rest of our lives. Things that would, for anyone else, illicit feelings of happiness can evoke dread or even terror.

Likewise, kindness and grace shown to us during moments of calamity and error seem to lessen the effect of our misfortune or mistakes. If deftly discerned, and faithfully acted upon, events that pose the risk of destroying our inner child, robbing from us innocence, optimism, and beauty, may be consumed in love—by Love's kind.

The Malones *were* Love's kind.

What the elders in the Malone family had astutely observed is that while all of us make mistakes, what distinguishes some from the masses is an ability to hold onto who they are, in spite of them.

Pink had made a dramatically terrible decision to shoot at the swarm of honeybees at the church, but Warner wanted to assure him that this action did not define him. The Malones had no way of knowing what words had been spoken over Pink in the few short years before he came to them, but they rightly assumed they were not kind. They were not there to witness his beatings, but they had seen the bruises firsthand and had decided to exempt the boy from certain accepted and routine forms of discipline in the family.

Warner had gotten a whuppin' or two in his youth, but he was never beaten or abused. He had spanked his own boys when necessary but carefully and thoughtfully. Corporal punishment was rarely his first choice when disciplining his boys, especially as they grew wiser and more resilient.

Warner was far too creative for that, so like his father and his father before him, he took the time and effort to teach more convincingly, than to simply just take off his belt. Once, when his boys were young, he'd asked Joe and CD to help him dig a drainage ditch off the side of one of their fields, to alleviate a systemic problem of flooding every time it rained. Not happy about such an arduous task, the two boys protested and complained for hours. Warner decided to teach them a lesson, they wouldn't soon forget.

The Lesson (August 1904)

Out in the hot sun with picks, shovels, and grubbin' hoes they labored to cut a seventy-five-foot trench on the side of the field. The two boys repeatedly voiced their unhappiness with being given the job. So, even though it doubled the time and effort to dig the ditch, Warner's approach toward disciplining them taught lasting lessons that other methods could not.

While they worked, Warner admonished Joe and CD to quit their bickering and complaining, but to no avail. The three of them were nearly half-finished with the task, when Warner had had enough of their griping.

Exasperated, he stood up and wiped the sweat from his brow. He pushed the blade of his shovel into the earth and left it standing on its own. He scratched his head, pretending to be concerned, and announced... "Boys, I think we've made a mistake. This ditch needs to be five more feet closer to the tree line. We'll have to move it."

Now, one might ask, how a person would go about moving a ditch. It is a fair question, with a simple answer. One must fill in the ditch they have already dug and then dig a new one in a different place.

"This is going to set us back on the day a good bit, so while you two fill this ditch in, I'll go up to the house and knock out a few chores. I'll come back in a couple of hours to help you finish up the new one."

Joe and CD watched as Warner walked toward the barn grove. Fortunately, they couldn't see the giant grin on their daddy's face, as he'd given them ample warning and plenty of opportunity to find a better attitude and quit their complaining. Now, they would learn the lesson "Adam's way" as Warner called it, by the sweat of their brow.

When their daddy had walked out of earshot, CD threw his shovel down on the ground in anger.

"Gol'Dangit Joe, we'll be here all day now!" he shouted. "Sometimes I wish he'd just whup us and get it over with."

Joe walked over, picked up CD's shovel, handed it to his brother, and said, "Well, I reckon the only way out of this now, is to get to work."

Sometime in the afternoon, after Pink's "emergency evacuation" at the church prayer meeting, tiny raindrops began to fall softly. And seemingly, out of nowhere, storm clouds blew in from the west over Massanutten Mountain, and for the first time in a month and a half, it began to rain. It was a perfect rain for watering the earth. Sometimes rain comes down so hard and fast that it runs over the ground, peeling away valuable topsoil and taking with it crops and nutrients, leaving behind great scars and lost revenue. This rain came down like a gentle gift. It was what the old folks called "a good soakin' rain". The ground was dry and thirsty, and it drank up every drop. The rains came down steady and light for almost three full days. By the end of the week, everything was looking brighter. The corn plants had greened up again and their leaves uncurled. Wilted cotton plants were standing once again, straining toward the sun. Everyone in the community was so happy about the rain that they had almost forgotten about the bees.

Almost.

The rain had postponed Warner's plan to take Pink fishing to talk about what had happened earlier in the day, but before he left CD and Leola's place, he had assured them both that the matter would keep.

By the following Sunday, the rains had passed, and new hope and optimism for the crops filled the community. However, the first Sunday back in the church *after the honeybee incident* was somewhat awkward for CD, Leola, and Pink, but not nearly as much as it was for Pastor Donnie Briscoe. In fact, his face blushed bright red for the first five minutes of his sermon. The residual smell of the brimstone and alcohol mixture, that had been burned to fumigate the church, lingered as a reminder of the chaos Pink had caused. Sister Clara was noticeably absent that day. Unlike Donnie, she did not work at the church and could therefore remain home until her dignity had returned. When the service was over, everyone shook the parson's hand as they exited the sanctuary. "That was a fine message, Pastor," offered CD as they stepped outside. "I wanted to apologize for my boy and offer to pay for anything that was damaged."

"Well," blushed Pastor Briscoe, "I suppose it was all harmless enough in the end. I've wondered all week if the bees swarming into the church lent everyone to more...let's say, urgent prayer. Who knows, that might even be the reason for our relief from this drought."

Leola smiled nervously, "I would have to agree with you. There were probably a lot more prayers going up at that moment than usual."

The pastor, CD, and Leola had a cordial conversation and in the end, laughed the whole matter off as innocent childhood mischief, but even so, Pink hid behind his mother's dress the whole time.

Up until this point, there really hadn't been any punishment for Pink's "indiscretion", so naturally Pink was a little wary, waiting for the other shoe to drop.

That afternoon, everyone gathered at Warner and Mary Ethel's house for Sunday dinner. Even CD contributed, making a batch of his famous black-bottomed biscuits.

After everyone had eaten, Warner asked Pink if he would like to ride out to Uncle's Jim's place and try their luck at the pond.

"Mama, can I go with Granddaddy, please?" asked Pink.

Leola was pleased that Warner had not forgotten about his promise to speak with Pink. "I think that is a wonderful idea," she replied. "About what time do you expect to be back?"

Pink looked at his grandpa for an answer.

"I reckon we ought to be home in time for supper. We might even have a couple of fish to add to the grease," replied Warner.

Pink jumped up and heading outside, hollered, "I'll go scratch us up some worms."

While Pink was outside digging for worms at the hog parlor, Warner, Mary Ethel, CD, and Leola planned out how they thought the conversation about the honeybees should go. As they continued to discuss the lessons that Pink needed to be taught, Leola became quiet and almost withdrawn from the conversation.

Noticing her distraction, CD asked, "Is everything alright?"

Leola looked at Warner and reached across the table, taking his hand in hers. Her eyes moistened, and she opened her mouth to speak, but hesitated.

Mary Ethel moved her chair closer to Leola's and put an arm around her shoulder. "What is it dear?" she asked.

Making another attempt, Leola looked at Warner and said, "You're the one who found Pink. You're the reason he came to us, and I think it's time Pink knows where he came from."

"What are getting at?" asked CD.

Leola let go of Warner's hand and shifted in her chair. She looked intently at CD and smiled. "I think your father should be the one to tell Pink how he came to us, and I think it should be today. I don't know how I know this, but I know."

Mary Ethel squeezed Leola's shoulders together in a hug, got up to fetch a pitcher of sweet tea, and said, "You boys mind what she says now. Some things a mother just knows."

Mary Ethel's words sunk deep into Leola's heart. She'd struggled to feel like a real mother since she hadn't come by motherhood, in the traditional way. Mary Ethel's affirmation carried weight and made her feel like a true peer among mothers. Turning back to CD, she asked, "Do you trust me?"

"Yes, of course, I trust you sweetheart," replied CD.

"Then it's settled. Warner, would you mind telling Pink that we adopted him, but we love him as much as if he was our own blood kin?" asked Leola.

Warner smiled at his daughter-in-law. He thought to himself, *"What a blessing this woman is to our family and especially to Pink."* Warner loved all of his grandchildren, but Pink had given him something extra. How everyone in the Malone family had completely loved and accepted Pink, made him proud of the way he and Mary Ethel had brought up their children. He'd always considered that they had raised a fine family, but the space they had carved out in their hearts for Pink was proof.

Warner agreed to Leola's request and together the four of them discussed what he should say to break the news to the boy, as gently as possible. When it was time to leave for Jim's place, Warner stepped outside to find that Pink already had two cane poles and a coffee tin full of worms in the back of the wagon, and he'd even led Molly out from the barn around to the tack shed.

"Alright, alright, I'm coming," laughed Warner.

It was a forty-five minute ride out to Jim's place. On the way, Warner did his best to explain to Pink the serious nature of what he'd done at the church concerning the bees. He took his time, carefully discussing the matter, but under the looming shadow of what he knew he would soon have to tell him, it seemed rather trivial.

"What were you thinking when you shot those bees?" he asked.

"Jimmy said I couldn't hit 'em from where we were standin'— so I showed him," declared Pink.

Warner chuckled. All he could think was that he'd have probably done the same thing at his age.

Growing up is a difficult process. It's plenty tough for the wise, even tougher for fools. But then there's a group that falls in between, neither wise nor foolish, who must learn from both.

"Pink, what do *you* think about shooting the bees?" asked his grandpa.

Pink answered the question quickly and confidently, "I think it was a perfect shot... dirt-n-all!"

Warner smiled, "What I mean is, what are your thoughts about the whole matter? Do you think it was a good or bad idea?"

"Bad," replied the boy.

Warner asked Pink what he would change about the event if he could. Pink's answer made him laugh, "I'd make them bees swarm someplace besides over the window of the church."

In short order, Warner felt that Pink understood his mistake and the matter was dropped.

When they arrived at Jim's place, they went up to the house to say hello. After a short visit, Jim offered to water Molly and let her graze upon some of the apples that had fallen from the tree, while Warner and Pink walked down to the pond.

When they had baited their hooks and set their lines out, Warner began the talk he'd been rehearsing on the ride over to Jim's place.

Warner and Pink were sitting in the grass by the pond under a sycamore tree. It was the only tree on that side of the pond. It was a large tree that gave plenty of shade. He moved over next to Pink, put his arm around him, and pulled him close.

"Pink, you know I love you don't you?" asked Warner.

Pink was sitting with his knees bent. He was holding his fishing pole with both hands, resting them on his knees.

Staring at the grass between his feet, he mumbled his answer, "Yes, sir."

Warner continued to beat around the bush, as he struggled to make himself say the words. Even at his young age, Pink could sense that his grandpa was trying to tell him something, and whatever it was... it wasn't good.

The longer Warner took to get to the point, the more anxiety and grief took hold of Pink's little heart. In his imagination, he had already figured out what his granddaddy was struggling to tell him.

Finally, his grandpa just blurted it out.

"Pink, what I need to tell you is that we adopted you into this family. When you were about four, or so, Edward and I were coming back from town and we found you wandering up the road, at night, in the rain."

Pink looked up at Warner. His expression was confused. Puzzled by his grandfather's words, he started to cry.

Warner's heart sank. What he had feared most was happening. It was too soon in Pink's life and the news was hurting the boy. "Pink, we all love you, son. Don't ever doubt that. Your mama and daddy, and all of us, love you as much as anyone else in the family," he explained.

Warner was doing his best to assure the boy that everything would be all right, when out of nowhere, Pink turned and barked, "I already know I don't belong here!"

Warner was stunned silent. He let go of Pink and knelt in front of him. "What do mean, you don't belong here?"

"I remember when you found me. I remember running away from Ricky and Sue when the train stopped! They hated me, and now everyone here hates me on account of what I done, and you tricked me into comin' out here to Uncle Jim's place, where the train goes through, just so you can put me back on it and make me go away!" yelled Pink, without taking a breath.

He was crying and talking so fast Warner could barely make out what he was saying. It shocked him to hear names associated with his abusers. It hurt him, to his heart, to know that his beloved grandson could still feel so much of the pain and anger.

His head spinning and his chest tightening, Warner sat back in the grass, trying not to fall over.

"No... no... no... Pink, no I brought you out here to tell you that no matter what you ever say or do, you will always be loved in this family, because we *chose* you," Warner desperately explained.

Pink jumped up and scurried into the sycamore tree.

"It's not true!" shouted Pink. "Y'all are ashamed of me! I heard mama say it!"

Warner stood looking up at Pink, tears now streaming down his face. Pink's reaction had caught him completely off guard. He had no idea the boy had retained any recollection of the night he was found. His despondency and reluctance to speak for days after they brought him home, had given everyone the impression that he would soon forget the whole matter.

An awful thing about trauma though, it's hard to forget. Even if we cannot recall the details, years later, we find ourselves acting out of the damage it caused so long ago.

Pink had not forgotten. Some of the details were fuzzy and dim, but the feelings and the fear were still clear. He couldn't remember the hurtful names he'd been called by his kidnappers, but he could still hear their angry tone.

The bruises on his body had healed, but the wounds that penetrated to his soul remained. Warner's unconditional love had touched those wounds, and Pink reacted the only way he knew how—he ran.

Plenty of children have run away and for many different reasons. Pink had successfully escaped from the people who were abusing him the night he came to the Malones, but then again he hadn't gone up a tree either.

All he wanted was to run away, but he'd made a critical miscalculation when he shimmied up the tree. With his grandpa standing right under it, there was no chance for escape.

"Come down outta that tree, Pink. Let's go home. We can talk this over some more on the ride home, and then we can discuss it with your mama and daddy."

Pink was now crying so hard his little body began to quiver and shake. Warner worried that he might lose his grip and fall.

Off in the distance, a train sounded its whistle.

Chapter 8

Choices

We all make choices every day. Whether it's what to wear, what to eat, or what to say, it's a sure bet we make hundreds of small decisions daily. As adults, we make some decisions that affect the lives of others. Small choices are of little consequence, but the big ones bear so much freight, we are wise to take them seriously. And part of growing up is learning to make choices that are wise and beneficial. It is rare for young children to face big decisions that will have lifelong consequences. But sometimes...

The following morning, when the sun crept over Hawksbill Mountain, light filled the valley. In the first moments of dawn, life-giving sunshine opened flowers, awakened birds, and began to warm the soil.

Sunlight warmed Warner's face and stirred him awake. His back was so stiff, he wondered if he'd be able to get up off the ground. His eyes opened, he struggled to focus, then he discovered that someone had thrown a quilt over him in the night.

"*Good old Jim*," he thought to himself and then something stirred against his chest.

Peeling back the blanket, he looked down. Pink was asleep across his lap, with his head resting against his chest, and his arms around him.

The boy had caught him sleeping. Warner had camped out under the sycamore tree all night, so that he could intercept Pink when he finally climbed down, but he had fallen asleep.

Pink could have easily made his escape, and his grandfather knew it—but the boy chose to stay. Pink had come into the Malone family because they had chosen him. And during the night, up in that sycamore tree, Pink chose them back.

It was a watershed moment for Pink and his grandfather. Warner wept softly and quietly... precious tears of relief and joy fell from his eyes and baptized the boy in assurance. Love washed over him, as only it can, onto Love's kind. He said a short prayer, thanking the Lord for keeping them through the night.

For another half hour, Warner sat perfectly still, doing his best not to disturb the boy's sleep. All the while, his back ached and prodded him to stand and stretch, but he dared not move.

After a few minutes, he could hear footsteps, in the tall grass, coming down from the house. He thought it must be his brother, but when Leola spoke, he remembered that she must have been worried sick when they didn't come home the previous night.

"Well, good morning you two," greeted Leola, "decide to have a little campout did you?"

Warner smiled and whispered, "I'm real sorry. Things got a little out of hand yesterday, but I think everything's going to be okay now."

Just behind Leola, CD came down the hill with Uncle Jim. He'd walked alongside Warner's brother, who was much older, to help him navigate the overgrown hillside.

When they were all together, Warner filled them in on all that had happened the day before. He explained that Pink had imagined that he'd brought him to Jim's place, to put him on another train and send him away. He told them about Pink climbing the sycamore tree and refusing to come down.

Warner looked at CD and said, "This boy's as stubborn as you. He climbed this tree nearly to the top and refused to come down, so I sat down under it and refused to leave."

Leola shook her head in disbelief and replied, "You sat there all night?"

Nodding his head, Warner replied, "I told him I could sit on the ground a whole lot longer than he could sit in a tree and that when he got tired of runnin', I'd be right here waitin'. When I woke up, I had a quilt and your boy asleep in my lap."

Jim chuckled, "I heard almost every word of the yelling and screaming last night. Sound carries uphill from water, you know. Some time or another I fell asleep in my chair, on the porch. After a while, I woke up and could see you in the moonlight, still under the tree. I didn't know if you were alive or dead, so I went to check on you and took a blanket with me, just in case you needed it. When I got down to where you were, the boy was already curled up in your lap."

Warner gave his brother a smile. Jim had always looked out for Warner and the others.

He looked down and thought he caught Pink staring up at him, but the boy shut his eyes tight and pretended to be asleep.

Warner smiled at Leola and said, "He told me last night that he wanted to go away for good and never come back." He paused to catch his breath and take control of his emotions, "I'd rather be in hell with my back broke, than to see this boy gone from our family!" His voice quivering, the words came out of Warner's mouth slow and choppy. He felt Pink squeeze his arms tighter around him. He looked down and Pink was now grinning from ear to ear.

Pink sat up, rubbed the sleep from his eyes, and then turned to his mother and father. "I'm real sorry about the bees. I didn't mean to shame our family."

Leola knelt beside him and took him into her arms. She hugged him so tight, the boy let out a loud groan. He laughed and so did everyone else.

"Only a mother can give a hug like that," said Warner.

Jim let everyone know that he was ready to head back up to the house. His bad hip was achin' him something fierce. He suggested they go inside and stir up something to eat.

"Well, look here. I set my traps yesterday. I baited them with fresh apples and a few radishes. Pink, if you and your daddy will go check my rabbit gums for me, you might find us something to eat for breakfast," he said.

"Well boy, you wanna go help me check the rabbit gums?" asked CD.

"Yes, sir!" replied Pink enthusiastically.

Warner left for a spell on the wagon, to go fetch Mary Ethel. He figured she'd be fit to be tied at his not coming home the night before. It wasn't the first time he'd been out all night, but without any advanced notice, he knew she would have sat up much of the night. Still, he rested knowing how she adored Pink and trusted that when she heard what had happened; she'd be quick to forgive.

CD and Pink found three plump rabbits and let one go. Two rabbits were enough, and one of the best ways to preserve meat, is to leave it alive.

Warner and Mary Ethel got back, just as the rabbit stew was coming out of the oven. They ate together and talked about this and that. Pink sat in his granddaddy Warner's lap almost the whole morning.

Warner, Pink, CD, Leola, and Mary Ethel spent the rest of the day at Jim's eating laughing, fishing, and playing games.

Warner's love and fidelity had changed something in the boy's heart. He had been set free to *be* a Malone. His grandfather had given him permission to choose love. It was real for him now.

Pink had chosen well.

Chapter 9

Get Up

"*It's morning, finally!*" thought Pink.

It was a day he'd anticipated for years on that farm and today was the day.

Pink's family had a two-mule farm, but being that his pa was the only man on the farm, just one of the mules was ever put to work at any given time. Pink had pestered his daddy to teach him how to drive the other mule for a good while, and CD had finally decided that Pink was old enough to learn. He was eleven years old now, and had gone through a bit of a growth spurt back in the fall. He was four feet, ten and a half inches tall and weighed about 90 pounds. Pink had a sharp mind, a quick wit, and he could think fast on his feet. So his daddy figured it was time to put that other mule to work, and Pink would be the man behind the plow.

It was a clear morning in late April 1921, and the sun was just creeping over the Blue Ridge. Warmth and light were spilling into the valley. The ground had dried from the late winter rains, and it was time to begin turning over the soil for the coming spring plant.

Pink lay awake in his bed as he stared at the ceiling and wondered about the day. He could smell biscuits, bacon, and coffee. His mother had been up for an hour or so to stoke the wood stove and start breakfast. The anticipation of the day nearly overwhelmed him. He rolled over, reached under the bed, and fumbling around, found the old cracker box where he kept his personal treasures.

Pulling the box up onto the bed, he dumped its contents. There was an arrowhead he'd found at Granddaddy Warner's place, a wooden ball, a brand-new pencil, and a handful of marbles. There was also a postcard with a picture of a train on it. The card had never been posted in the mail and Pink was quite proud of it. He'd purchased it at Floyd's Grocery with a penny he'd gotten for his birthday. He was fascinated by trains and terrified of them at the same time. He often stood mesmerized whenever they passed by on the rail line that ran through his Uncle Jim's place. Pink studied the postcard for a minute and then put the contents back inside the box, slid it under his bed, and lay back down. He placed his hands behind his head on the pillow and smiled.

"I almost forgot," he said aloud. "Sorry Lord, I'm just so excited that I get to plow today." Pink had been taught to start his day with prayer, and sometimes he even remembered to do it. He lay there a minute more thinking about what to say, before he carefully spoke, "Lord, I gotta mighty big day ahead of me. Today my daddy is gonna teach me how to drive a mule.

I don't want to let him down or make him think I'm too young to handle myself behind a plow. Help me be strong all day. In Jesus name, Amen."

This *was* a big day for Pink. Ever since he was a small boy, he'd followed his daddy around the farm. As he grew, he began to help more, so naturally, his daddy gave him more responsibilities and chores. Pink thought the world of his father and loved every minute they spent together working that land.

CD was already outside feeding the animals and getting a few things prepared for the day's work. He finished up and came back inside the house. "Good morning, darling. Did you sleep well?" he asked Leola. She turned from the sink and gave him a hug. "I did sleep well, and you?" she asked.

"I slept like the dead," said CD. "Where's that boy?"

Leola smiled. She was as proud of Pink as any mother could be. "He's so excited, he can hardly stand himself. It's all he's talked about for weeks," she said. "I prayed this morning that you two would have a good day."

"I think he's ready, and I believe he'll do fine. He's as stubborn as any one of those two mules ever thought about being, so I'd wager they're as nervous as he is," said CD.

Leola smiled and turned back to her work. She opened the oven and removed a pan of golden brown biscuits. They were good and tall. CD could see the flakey layers and remarked, "Have mercy, those look delicious!"

Leola smiled and said, "Well do me a favor and butter these, wrap them in a cloth, and place them in a basket."

CD took the pan, carefully smeared a dab of butter on each biscuit, and placed them in a basket lined with a piece of cloth.

When they were all buttered, he folded the cloth over them to keep them warm.

"Are you about ready to eat?" he asked Leola.

"Yes, you can call Pink to the table," she replied.

CD hollered out to Pink, and he wasn't more than a minute getting to the table. Already dressed, he was wearing bib over-alls, a white cotton shirt, and a well-worn pair of brogans. He sat down at the table and smiled so big it almost made his mother laugh with glee.

"Are you all ready to become a real plow boy?" asked Leola.

Pink nodded and opened his mouth to speak, but his pa interrupted. "He's about to become a plow *man*," proclaimed his proud father.

"I sure am!" exclaimed Pink. "I could hardly sleep last night, just thinking about it."

CD and Leola exchanged a look that communicated how proud they were of the boy.

"Which mule do I get, Daddy?" asked Pink.

"Well, which one do you want?" replied CD.

Pink thought for a moment and said, "I don't reckon I know exactly. The nicest one I suppose...maybe Jupiter."

Leola chuckled and said, "I'm sure your daddy will give you the most amiable mule—if there is such a thing."

CD got up from the table, walked over to the woodstove, and picked up the coffee pot. Pouring another cup, he said, "Well ol' Jupe is a hard-working mule, but Mars is a little easier to handle. Maybe it's best if we start you out with her."

"Yes, sir," came Pink's reply, "I reckon that's best."

Leola smiled and stood up to clear the table. She took Pink's plate and kissed the top of his head.

"Well, Son, it's almost seven o'clock. We have a lot to get done today. Let's get to work," said CD.

Pink stood up, put on his cap, and said, "Yes, sir."

CD picked up his pocketknife off the side table and dropped it in the front pocket of his britches. Pink noticed and smiled. He already had his pocketknife. He patted his left pocket and proceeded to quote a phrase CD had taught him since he was small, "A man ain't dressed without a pocketknife," he recited.

"You got that right," said his father.

When CD and Pink walked out to the mule barn, Jupiter and Mars were done eating their hay and were grazing on what grass they could eat by reaching their heads under the bottom rail of the fence. As they approached, Jupiter walked away, while Mars walked over to greet them.

Her easy demeanor reassured Pink. He put out a hand and stroked her face. CD already had the harness on her, and together he and Pink led Mars out to the edge of the field where the plow was waiting.

In only a minute or two, Mars was hitched to the plow and began stamping her feet. She was ready to go, ready to work, and impatiently waiting for the signal to... "Get up!"

CD motioned for Pink to take his place behind the plow and

said, "Well, Son, working a mule ain't easy. A mule is a stubborn animal."

Pink followed his daddy's statement with a question, "How come we plow with mules instead of an ox... like in Bible times?"

"You never want to plow with an ox," replied CD, "If you fall on hard times you might be tempted to eat the ox."

Grinning, Pink walked over and placed his hands on the plow the way he'd seen his father do, so many times before. He wasn't quite tall enough to comfortably maneuver the handles the way his daddy did, so CD showed Pink how to grip them from underneath with the handles over his shoulders.

"This looks dumb, don't it?" Pink asked.

"Not at all, Son. You don't ever look dumb doing honest work, at least not to the folks who matter," replied his daddy.

Pink smiled. His father's reassurance gave him confidence, and he turned back to the task at hand. He took a half-step back with his right leg and pushed up on the plow. He lifted it a bit, to show his dad that he was strong enough. CD placed a hand on his shoulder and knelt down beside him. He picked up the reins that were draped across the braces of the plow handles and gave them to Pink.

"Alright," CD began, "when she starts, the plow might jerk to one side or the other, until she pulls it straight. That's okay, you don't have to do anything except hold the plow and keep the reins even and a little loose."

Pink was nervous but intent on not showing it.

"Okay, whenever you're ready," said his father.

Pink took a deep breath and strengthened his grip on the

handles. "Get up!" he said with a loud firm tone. He put the emphasis on the "u" in "up" because his daddy had taught him that work animals key in on the vowel sounds in the commands. It is for this reason that mule driving requires the use of the words "gee" and "haw". These commands for right and left respectively, have distinct vowel sounds.

The plow lurched and then straightened, just as his father said it would. At the end of the row, Pink called to the mule, "Whoa!" and she came to a stop. Looking back at the line he and Mars had carved in the soil, Pink was disappointed, "It's pretty crooked, ain't it Daddy?"

CD got down on one knee, stretched out his arm, and stuck up his thumb to sight down the row Pink had plowed. "Well, it's crooked alright, but not nearly as crooked as my first row was when I was your age," he assured.

Pink's heart swelled. "Let's go again!" he shouted eagerly.

CD showed him how to turn the mule and plow around for another pass, and again, Pink called out, "Get up!"

Just a few paces into the row, Mars stopped. "Get up!" said Pink. Mars made no move, nor any sign that she intended to ever go again. Pink deepened his voice thinking that it might help if he sounded more like his daddy. "Get up!" he said, almost screaming, but Mars stood her ground.

"Well, she does that sometimes," said CD. He walked around her and balled up his fist. Pop! CD hit Mars lightly, right between the eyes, and immediately she was ready to work again.

"Every once in a while, she'll act up on you and that there is the only fix I've found," explained his father.

Leola could see them from the kitchen window. It warmed her heart to see Pink learning to handle a plow and work like a man.

She'd fretted over Pink's development at every stage. Not knowing where he came from or from what family stock, she lacked some of the clues others around might have had while predicting how their children would turn out. Pink, however, had impressed her at every turn and exceeded almost every expectation.

As Leola watched CD and Pink together, her heart felt full. As long as she could remember, she had daydreamed about being a mom. She'd come to believe that it wasn't the Lord's plan for her to bear children, but Pink was just as much hers, as if she had carried him to term. The way he treated Pink, made Leola love CD all the more. She knew that CD had come from a strong family and had assumed he would make a good father, but she never dreamed he would be so wonderful at being a dad.

A few hours later CD and Pink came back up to the house for dinner. They were both dirty and sweaty. Pink stomped his feet on the back porch and tried to kick off as much dirt as possible.

CD noticed Pink attempting to knock the dirt from his shoes. "When I was your age, your Granddaddy Warner used to say 'It's not dirt until it gets on mama's rugs,' When it's in the field it's soil. Dirt brings grief, but soil brings life," CD said.

Turning his feet over one at a time to get a better look, Pink examined the bottoms of his boots to be sure he wasn't about to track "grief" into the house.

When the pair came into the kitchen, Leola put two glasses of water on the table for them. "I saw you two men coming out of the fields and thought you might appreciate something to wash away the dust," she said.

"Right as usual," said CD, picking up his glass and drinking it down.

Pink was beside himself with joy. The day was as fulfilling as any day had ever been. He was going through a rite of passage and it felt amazing. His daddy was treating him like a peer and what's more, his mother had just called him a man.

Pink sat at the table with one leg out beside his chair and one hand on his hip, a near carbon copy of his pa. He loved his family and he loved being a part of it.

The smell of chicken stew filled the kitchen. A large pot sat on the stove and great heaps of steam billowed from it. Leola had butchered an old hen that had quit laying eggs, and she was putting together a stew around it. In the pot were tomatoes, butter beans, and cabbage from last year's canning, as well as some potatoes and carrots from the root cellar. She had even snuck in a small piece of fatback, to give the old bird a bit of flavor.

CD walked over to the stove and lifting the lid on the pot asked, "What's the main attraction in this stew?"

"Chicken," came Leola's reply.

"I see," said CD. "Where'd we get a chicken for the stew pot?"

Leola smiled, she appreciated CD's careful stewardship over what the Lord had given them. Times were hard and resources were scarce, so every morsel of meat had to be carefully rationed and accounted for. Leola and CD were a perfect match and made a good team.

"Father Time gave us this bird," she said.

CD looked at Pink and with a playful tone said, "Don't ever grow old around here Son, or you'll end up in the stewpot!"

Pink smiled, and Leola swatted at CD with a hand towel.

"Your daddy is too tenderhearted to kill the fowl on this farm when they age out of egg-laying," explained Leola, "so I do it."

She dished up the stew into three bowls, and one at a time, set them on the table. From the pie safe she produced a basket of cornbread she'd made earlier in the morning. Pink's face lit up. Cornbread was his favorite. He reached into the basket and found a corner piece. He always tried to get a corner piece because it had twice as much crust around the top than the others.

The stew was good but not delicious. Old hens are usually quite tough and a stew is about all that they are fit for. The fatback helped and when CD found it in his bowl, he fished it out with his fork and gave it to Pink.

"Here Son, you better take this piece of pork. It'll give you more energy for the rest of the day," said CD.

Pink had a mouthful of stew and cornbread but managed a smile. He swallowed and said, "Thank you, Daddy. What are we doing next?"

CD looked at Leola and asked, "Is there anything you need help with dear?"

"Well no, not around the house anyway, but I would like to cook up a mess of fish for supper. I don't suppose you and Pink could go down to Uncle Jim's and catch me some?" she replied smiling.

"Yippee!" exclaimed Pink.

"Well, it's two o'clock and we still have a few things to button up around here. It probably won't be more than a half-hour, and we can leave for Uncle Jim's place," CD explained.

Pink and CD got up from the table and started out the back door. Leola called out, "Now y'all don't be too long. I want to have supper around 6:30."

CD, already out on the porch, hollered, "Yes Ma'am."

Chapter 10

Overwhelmed

P ink and his daddy saddle soaped the mule harness, threw a few forks of hay into the mule pen, moved the milk cow so she would have some new grass to eat, and slopped some potatoes that had gone bad to the hogs.

At the hog parlor, Pink used a pitchfork to turn the soil over. "Phew wee!" he exclaimed. The smell of hog manure filled the air and his nostrils objected. The ground was crawling with red wiggler earthworms. He reached over to grab the old coffee can they kept on a fence post. He scooped up a handful of worms and dropped them into the can.

"That's a plenty," said CD.

Pink smiled, "Better to have and not need, right?"

His father, nodding his head, replied, "Always."

After a while, CD pushed the old T-model Ford out from under a shed and Pink hopped in the driver's seat. His daddy had taught him how to start the car, but he lacked the strength to turn the crank, so he busied himself with the other tasks associated with getting the engine started.

Pink grabbed the hand lever with both hands, and with a loud grunt, he pulled it all the way back. Next, he set the spark advance all the way to the top and adjusted the throttle to about one quarter of the way open.

"You all set in there?" asked CD.

Pink pulled himself up high with the steering wheel so that he could see out of the windscreen and over the hood. "Yes, sir," he shouted.

"Is the key switch off?" asked CD.

"Yes, sir," called out Pink.

CD turned on the fuel valve and rotated the engine crank exactly four times to prime the engine with fuel. Pink was following along in his mind. He had memorized every complicated step in starting that car. He knew that what came next, was the most dangerous part... turning the crank with the key switch on. His hand was already on the switch anticipating the command he knew was coming.

"Okay, light her up," said CD.

Pink turned the key switch to the "Run" position, and with his left hand, CD gave the crank a few quick flips until the engine sputtered. As soon as Pink heard the engine cough to life, he advanced the spark lever, like he'd been taught, and gave the engine a little more gas.

The old Model T spit and coughed a few times before the engine smoothed out and began to idle more evenly.

"Okay, that'll do it!" yelled CD over the noise of the engine. Pink slipped over to the other side of the car and CD got in under the wheel. "Let's go catch some fish," he said smiling at Pink.

"I bet it'll be a banner day for 'em," replied the boy.

As they turned off the good road, down the path toward Uncle Jim's house, they could see the small lake down the hill. It was glassy smooth and the sun was glistening off the surface. "I hope they're hungry," said Pink.

Pink asked his daddy if he could sound the horn and CD obliged him. Pink pushed on the plunger hard and fast, several times.

"I reckon that's enough. He'll know we're comin'," said CD

When they rounded the path behind the house, Uncle Jim was already coming out the back door. "Well, looky here. What's the occasion?" he asked.

Pink was first out of the car. He ran over and put out his hand. Uncle Jim looked perplexed and glanced over at CD with a quizzical look on his face. CD smiled and gave Uncle Jim a wink.

Uncle Jim shook Pink's hand, and then used his grip him to yank him into a hug. Pink laughed and said, "Well, I wanted to shake your hand, on account of I'm a man now."

Uncle Jim raised his eyebrows and feigned surprise, "A man? Well, now tell me when did this happen?" he said playfully.

CD had squared away the car, set the hand lever by now, and walked over to Uncle Jim to shake his hand.

"It's good to see you, Uncle Jim," said CD. His uncle nodded his head.

CD stepped over to Pink and put his arm around his shoulder. With a beaming smile he said, "Pink's learning to plow."

This time, Uncle Jim was genuinely surprised. He took a step backward and rubbed his chin. He stood there examining Pink before he spoke, "Yes siree, I can definitely see it. You've grown a heap, and it looks like you've put on a fair amount of muscle too."

Pink smiled wide and proud.

"You ain't afraid of them mules?" asked Uncle Jim. "You know one good kick from a mule can cripple a man, maybe even send him off to the Promised Land."

"No sir, I ain't afraid, one bit. My daddy says I'm a natural at handlin' that mule," replied Pink.

Uncle Jim mussed his hair and said, "I bet you are. Now did you boys ride all the way out here to tell me that or is there something else?"

"Mama sent us over here to get a mess of fish for supper," explained Pink.

"Well, you picked a perfect time. The fish are bitin' so good, I'm scared to dip a toe in the water for fear of losin' it," Uncle Jim replied.

"Oh, boy!" exclaimed Pink.

Uncle Jim smiled, pointed to the lake and said, "Right down there by the sycamore tree, you'll find a couple of cane poles. You go get started. I have something to talk to your daddy about."

CD looked at Pink and said, "Go on ahead Son, I'll be down there directly."

Pink fetched the coffee can of red wigglers from the car and then ran the entire way down to the small lake.

Uncle Jim motioned for CD to sit in one of the two chairs on the back porch. CD chose an old Windsor chair that looked a little suspect. It was weathered and well worn. He picked it up as if to reposition it, but really, he was trying to determine if it was sound enough to hold his weight. Satisfied it was solid enough, he sat down, crossed his ankle over one knee, and looked out at the landscape. He spotted Pink down at the pond, he was already minding two fishing poles that he'd set out with bait. The view from the porch was spectacular.

Uncle Jim's place was around three hundred acres. Mostly forested with hardwood trees, it had about fifty acres of fields that were suitable for farming. Down in a little draw, he had created a pond by damming up a humble stream that wound its way through the place. His house wasn't much. It was a simple one-room shack with a sink, table, bed, and a woodstove. It wasn't suitable for a family, but Uncle Jim had never married, so it was perfect for him. The back porch was large and had a nice railing. He spent a good deal of time out there in the evenings, smoking his tobacco pipe and playing his guitar. To Uncle Jim, his property was a little piece of paradise.

CD and Uncle Jim sat in silence for a spell, while Jim collected his thoughts.

Uncle Jim lit his pipe and took a deep draw to establish the fire. He tamped the tobacco gently with his Barlow knife and clamped it in his teeth. With the pipe in the corner of his mouth, he announced, "You know, I aim to give him this place someday."

CD had a look of shock on his face. He put all four legs of the chair back on the floor and sat up straight. He raised a hand as if to say "stop" and began to object, "Uncle Jim, that's mighty generous of you, but I don't think…"

Uncle Jim interrupted, "That ain't for no one to decide but me. Pink is my nephew, he's gonna be a fine man someday, and if I want to leave this piece of land to him, well, that's my business. Besides, a man wants to know that when he's gone, the land he loved will be taken care of and cherished."

CD lowered his head and stared at the porch floor for a moment. It overwhelmed his heart to know that his Uncle Jim loved Pink so much, as to give him his place.

He looked up at his Uncle Jim and smiling said, "Yes, sir. I know Pink will take care of it."

Standing up, CD reached out to shake his Uncle's hand. Jim held his grip a little longer than usual and looked CD in the eye. "There's something really special about that boy, and I know he didn't find his way into this family by accident. This has the Lord's mark all over it," he said.

"You sound just like Leola," CD said laughing.

Jim laughed and did his best courtesy.

CD and Uncle Jim turned their attention back to Pink. He was distracted away from the fishing poles and was half way up the sycamore tree.

"Reckon what he's doing up that tree again?" asked Uncle Jim.

CD looked at Uncle Jim and grinned. "C'mon," he said, "Pink has a knack for finding interesting things—*treasures* he calls them."

Jim and CD headed down the hill toward the tree. It was about two hundred yards or so from Uncle Jim's house to the lake, so it took a few minutes for them to reach Pink. Uncle Jim was in his mid-sixties, and his walking pace had slowed quite a bit. He'd had a stroke a few years back and the fact that he was walking at all had amazed everyone.

"You doing alright?" asked CD.

"Yep, I just have to take my time and mind that I don't put my foot wrong and fall. The doctor tells me broken bones heal up mighty slow in old folks," replied Uncle Jim.

CD hated hearing his Uncle declare himself old. He'd lionized him as a boy and had admired him his whole life.

"You ain't old," he assured, "You're just broken in good."

Uncle Jim let out a loud laugh, "Ha!" he said, "You're half-right."

The pair chuckled and travelled the last few yards down to the lake. When they got within earshot, Pink called out, "Y'all ain't gonna believe what I found." Pink said nothing else, purposefully leaving Uncle Jim and CD wondering in anticipation.

"Well, what is it?" hollered Uncle Jim.

"It's a great big Luna Moth. I'm trying to fetch it down," exclaimed Pink.

As they approached the lake, CD noticed that one of the

corks had disappeared. He reached down, picked up the cane pole, and retrieved a keeper-sized crappie. He strung it on the line Pink had staked to the shore. There were already about a half dozen huge slabs on the stringer.

"*Boy, Leola is gonna be so proud,*" he thought.

CD turned around just as Pink was jumping down from the lowest crotch in the tree. In his hand, he carefully cradled a bright green moth about five inches across. "She's beautiful!" said Pink, holding the moth up for Uncle Jim to see.

Uncle Jim leaned back a bit so his aged eyes could focus on the moth. "She sure is, Pink," he observed.

CD gave Pink a pat on the back and mussed his hair. He was proud of Pink's appreciation for nature and did not see his fascination with creation as a distraction. In fact, CD encouraged his curiosity about the world.

"I expect we ought to be heading home now. You've already caught enough fish for supper," said CD.

Pink gently placed the moth on the shaggy bark of the sycamore tree's trunk and replied, "Yes, sir."

"Why don't you come have supper with us Uncle Jim? There's plenty of fish for all of us and Leola would love to see you," offered CD.

Uncle Jim smiled but declined. "I don't think so, but thank you for the invite."

"I'd be happy to carry you on the car and then drive you home after supper," said CD.

"No thank you. I've got a squirrel stew in the house that I have on a simmer," explained Uncle Jim.

Pink took Uncle Jim's hand to steady him on the climb back

up the hill toward the house and CD carried the fish. Uncle Jim and Pink laughed and chided one another, about this and that, all the way back up to the house. CD kept a good distance so as not to intrude and marveled at how easily Pink could be himself around Uncle Jim. It made him love his family all the more. He also couldn't stop thinking about the enormous gift Jim would someday give to Pink.

It is said that one of the best ways to show love to another is to be kind to and love the ones they themselves care about. CD's admiration for Uncle Jim had increased ten-fold that afternoon. He glanced toward heaven and whispered, "Thank you."

Chapter 11

Enough?

A couple of weeks after Pink had his first lesson plowing with the mule, his daddy and his brothers made plans to go out of town to Charlottesville. They'd decided to go make some short money cleaning up a coal spill after a train derailment. There was plenty of speculation about what caused the train to come off its tracks and the C&O Railroad Company was busy investigating the matter.

Word came to CD, through a cousin who worked for the railroad, that over 1200 tons of coal had spilled out along the tracks near Charlottesville, VA, and a great many men were needed to recover it. CD and his two brothers, Joe and Ed'ard, were planning to take the train out of Luray on a Monday morning and were hoping to be home in about ten days. Rumor was that the job of shoveling up the loose coal paid four dollars a day. Money was scarce and this opportunity was too good to pass up. No one could tell how long the job would take, but it would be good money as long as it lasted.

"I reckon I'll need to be up around five in the morning," said CD. "I'll have my bag packed and a shovel to take in case they don't have one for me."

Pink stood up from his chair in the kitchen, "Daddy, please let me go with you. I know I'm small, but I can work all day and I'll be good help, I promise!"

"Pink, you're better help than most men in this valley, and that's exactly why I need you to stay here and mind this farm," said CD. "Every man wants to know his family and his property are going to be looked after when he's gone, and it gives me peace of mind knowing that I have you to see to it."

It wasn't the answer Pink wanted, but it was the one he expected. As badly as he wanted to go, he knew he was too young, and besides, it would be too much for his mama for both of them to be absent. Pink smiled at his daddy, struggling to keep the disappointment off his face.

CD leaned over to muss Pink's hair and then pulled him into a hug. As Pink wrapped his arms around his daddy, Leola came over and joined them.

Squeezing her husband and son tightly she sighed, "I do love these family hugs." She pulled her head away and looked down at Pink and said, "Son, I need a strong man around here to help me while your daddy is gone."

Pink smiled big. He appreciated the way his mother made such a deliberate effort to make him feel special and needed.

"C'mon," said Leola, "Let's make some popcorn on the stove.

Maybe your daddy will read to us from the Story Hour Reader?" She looked at CD and smiled.

"Oh, please Daddy?" pleaded Pink, "Read 'Pouchy Pelican' and 'Punchinello' they're my favorites."

"Alright, that sounds like a good idea. I'll fetch the book," replied CD.

He walked into the front room and stooped to look for the book on a small shelf where they kept the few they owned. From the kitchen, he could hear Pink and Leola laughing and carrying on about this and that. He tarried a while longer, soaking up the sounds of love.

"Are you alive in there darling?" called Leola from the kitchen.

"On my way!" replied CD.

Emerging from the front room, CD waved the book in the air as if he'd found a prize. CD and Leola had enjoyed reading to one another since they had first begun to court. It was a tradition taught to CD by his mother, and he and Leola had been diligent to continue it in their family.

Many nights Pink had fallen asleep in Leola's lap, while she or CD read to him. Reading books was important to their family, especially the Good Book. Often, they took turns reading. Whenever it was Pink's turn to read, he would make a big production of it. He would mimic the sounds of animals, deepen his voice while reading the parts spoken by men, and raise his pitch for the women. Pink loved to read, and he was good at it.

The three of them sat at the kitchen table around the oil

lamp. CD turned to page 179 in Coe and Christie's, *Story Hour Reader,* and he began:

Pouchy Pelican had worked very hard...

After the popcorn was all gone and several stories had been read, Pink was asleep at the table with his head resting in his folded arms.

CD stood up and closed the book. Placing it on the table, he whispered to Leola, "I'll carry him, you go turn down his bed."

Carefully, CD scooped Pink out of the chair and carried him to his room. Leola pulled off his socks and CD placed him on the bed and then tucked the covers up under his chin.

"He is the most beautiful thing I ever laid eyes on," said Leola with a song in her voice.

CD pulled her into a hug and looked her in the eye, "not me." He kissed Leola on the lips and she blushed.

"Not in front of the boy," she protested.

"Oh, he's fast asleep," replied CD, "Besides, it's good for a child to know his parents are in love."

Leola patted CD on the back, and the two returned to the kitchen to tidy up before bed. They washed the kettle and water glasses and then closed up the wood stove for the night, after CD added a large round piece of white oak to the fire.

The following morning the sun rose to find CD and Leola already up fixing breakfast together in the kitchen. Leola was humming softly, and CD was kneading biscuit dough.

He put the biscuits in the oven and added another stick of stove-wood to ensure they baked thoroughly.

"Look now," chided Leola, "You get that stove too hot and those biscuits will burn on the bottoms. The last time you got impatient with the biscuits, I used them as doorstops for a month!"

Laughing, CD replied, "I'll keep an eye on 'em."

Leola walked over, wrapped her arms around his waist, and laid her head on his chest. CD held her close and stroked her hair. He sensed what she was feeling. He felt it too. They had rarely been apart since their wedding twelve years ago.

"It's only a couple of weeks," whispered CD softly stroking her hair. "I'll send you a postcard from the train station in Charlottesville, as soon as I get there."

His promise comforted her, but still, her dread was too heavy to hide. Tears began to form in her eyes, and she wiped them with her apron.

"Charlottesville is a big city, full of worldly folk. I just want you home safe. That's all." Leola paused and turned toward the kitchen window so her husband could not see the fear on her face.

Fear is mighty powerful and often leads one to actions and words that make little sense to those not experiencing the same dread. In Leola's heart, she had never truly believed she was enough for CD, or anyone for that matter. She had always wondered, had there been more girls in their small rural community, if CD would have picked her above all the others. This self-doubt made her compare herself to almost every woman her age, though she tried not to show it.

Whether it was the way Leola would run herself down when she didn't think she was as pretty as the other women on Easter Sunday or how she'd compare her skills as a homemaker to her sisters or her mother-in-law, she unconsciously left clues about her deep fear.

CD was not the most observant man in the world, but this... this he'd noticed. Over the years, in small glimpses, he'd begun to piece together the way Leola doubted her beauty and worth, but today as he prepared to go off to the big city, he saw a more complete picture.

Squatting in front of the oven, CD carefully removed the biscuits. They were tall, fluffy, and somewhat blackened on the bottoms. Leola shot him an "I told you so" look and chuckled as she shook her head.

"I like 'em that way," CD teased. Then his tone became more serious, "Leola, I want you to know something... you are the most amazing woman in the world, and I know I ain't met all the women in the world, but I don't have to... some things a man just knows."

Setting the pan of biscuits on the counter, CD took her face in his hands. With his thumbs, he wiped the tears that were now streaming down her cheeks. "Leola, I believe the Lord brought us together, don't you?" he asked.

"Sure I do," she replied.

He slid his hands from her cheeks to her shoulders, "Well, do you think He ever gives us anything less than what's best?"

Leola knew he was right, but reality and truth often do little to stop us when we are succumbing to fear, and CD knew she wasn't convinced.

. . .

Suddenly, he grabbed her by the waist and taking her into his arms he lifted her off the floor and kissed her deep and long. It was as passionate a kiss, as ever there was! He squeezed her body tight and pressed her against the kitchen table, sending it sliding into the wall.

Leola pulled away breathless and stammered, "Charles Daniel! You better quit or you'll miss your train!"

"I need to give you *something* to keep me on your mind and in your heart while I'm away," replied CD.

Leola tried to smile, but the moment of their parting weighed on her, and her imagination pricked at her heart like so many needles.

"I just don't want some gussied-up city girl to steal you away from me," she said half joking.

And there it was... finally, in plain English. Her fear was personified in the imaginary woman who was just like all the others... more beautiful and capable than her, and more deserving of CD's love.

CD crossed his arms in front of his chest, "All the gold in California couldn't take me away from you."

"It ain't gold that worries me," she answered.

"Leola Reeves Malone, everything and everyone I could ever want or dream of is right here on this farm—except for Gerty. I would like to have a more agreeable milk cow," he said grinning.

Leola laughed, although half-hearted.

A horn sounded and looking out of the back kitchen window CD could see Ed'ard and Joe waiting in his T-model Ford. It was as dilapidated as a working automobile could get, but Joe only cared that it motored him around when he needed it to. With no heat, no doors or windows, and barely anything left of the top, it was still better than a buckboard because though both modes of transport were cold the automobile could make the trip sooner.

Picking up his bag, CD kissed Leola once more on the lips and then again on the forehead. He never left the farm, even just to run into town, without kissing her on the forehead. It was how he had kissed her for the first time, out behind Trinity Church when they were love-struck teenagers. His touch had always made Leola feel safe and loved, and though briefly, could chase away her fear.

"Tell, that boy that I am counting on him to tend to things while I'm gone. I'll write when I get to Charlottesville," said CD, as he walked off the back porch.

Leola stood at the door until Joe managed to get his automobile into gear and moving. She walked out into the yard and watched until the men were out of sight.

She clasped her hands and wrung them hard. Her fear had returned. Her fear was older than their love, and though not as strong, it was familiar and always present. The returning dread was not welcomed, so Leola said a short prayer... but in vain.

Chapter 12

Short Money

"I would like to purchase a ticket to Charlottesville please," said CD to the gentleman at the ticket counter.

"That'll be 65 cents, please," replied the man.

CD counted out the change and handed it to him. The ticket master took the money and gave him his ticket. CD reached for the ticket and taking it said, "Sure is cool weather for this late in April. We're goin' down to Charlottesville to make some short money cleanin' up that coal spill."

The man smiled, and looking past CD shouted, "Next!"

He noticed that the man was polite but not friendly. It was a little off-putting to CD. He was used to folks at least taking the time to carry on a little. He figured there were too many people waiting to buy tickets, for the man at the counter to talk to everyone, but still, CD thought it was a pity.

Joe and Ed'ard got their tickets and walked over to the platform to wait with all the other passengers for the train to arrive.

It was only a little past seven in the morning, but there were already a couple of dozen people waiting for the train. The first part of their journey would take them from Luray down to Waynesboro, where the three brothers would board another train the rest of the way over to Charlottesville.

The ride was beautiful, the spring redbuds and dogwoods were in full bloom. They passed big barns and lakes, and beautiful hillsides covered in new wildflowers and every so often they would get a glimpse of wisteria in full lavender display.

"The blossoms on those vines look almost like grapes, don't they?" asked Ed'ard.

Joe kicked his shoe and grinning replied, "Well, we'll come back after we make all this money and start us up a wine-makin' business."

"You mean a vineyard," corrected CD.

"Well, I forgot, we have a scholar in our midst. Tell us, how'd you come to know about vineyards? The only grapes you ever saw were scuppernongs on the banks of the Shenandoah," said Joe.

CD laughed and replied, "I reckon it's because I actually pay attention in church!" There was an accusation in his tone.

Ed'ard raised his hands in the air and whispered, "Amen!"

A few miles before the train arrived in Waynesboro, CD spied a meadow full of bluebells and trout lilies in full bloom. It looked as if someone had woven a giant carpet rug of blue and yellow flowers.

"Looky yonder," said CD. He pointed out of the window toward the meadow. "Those, right there, are the same flowers I picked to give Leola when I asked her to marry me. I'll never forget...my hands were so sweaty, the stems stained them green."

Ed'ard laughed, "You were no good the whole time you were courtin' that girl. You never showed up on time to help with chores, you skipped out on fishin'—the only thing you never missed was school and church because..." Joe joined him, and in unison, they said, "*that's where Leola was.*"

Smiling, CD proudly said, "I miss her already."

Across the aisle from the brothers, sat an older couple in their late 50's. The lady leaned into the aisle and asked, "Are you a newlywed, young man?"

Joe spoke up with laughter in his voice, "No ma'am he and Leola have been married over ten years. He's always carried on about her like that."

The lady acknowledged Joe, with a smile, and a nod and then turned to her husband and gave him a somewhat playful smack on the arm. Her husband leaned forward, and looking at Joe, Ed'ard, and CD, smiled while tipping his hat in a sarcastic "thank you".

CD shrugged his shoulders and whispered, "I can't help it."

At the Waynesboro station, the three of them decided to eat lunch at a café, a block or two down from the depot. They had their tickets and knew what time the train was due but still, CD was nervous.

"Let's get a bite to eat at that café over yonder. Leastways we can see in case the train gets here early," he said.

They each had a quarter budgeted, so they had to be careful ordering off the menu.

CD asked for a biscuit and a boiled egg, Ed'ard ordered pickled beets, a biscuit, and butterbeans, and Joe ordered a biscuit and a slice of cold ox tongue.

"I don't think I can eat with that cow tongue on your plate staring at me," said Ed'ard in disgust.

"Tongues don't stare, they lick," laughed Joe, picking up the slice of ox tongue on his fork and waving it at Ed'ard.

CD was already laughing. He'd seen the expression on Ed'ard's face when Joe ordered the tongue. Their waitress didn't even blink, when he said, "I'll have cold ox tongue," but Ed'ard sure did. His face looked like it might flip inside out.

CD waited in ambush for Joe to take the first bite. "What's it like havin' your food taste you back?" he snickered. Joe laughed out loud.

"Dadgummit!" snipped Ed'ard. "Are y'all gonna let me eat? We got a good ten days of hard laborin' to do, and we need to keep up our strength!"

When the men had finished their meal, they got up to afford the table to other hungry folk and walked back over to the station. They sat on the platform with their legs dangling off the edge.

"Train tracks sure are mysterious," mused CD.

"How do you mean?" asked Joe.

"Well, I guess I mean that you don't have no idea how far or where they go, by just sittin' here," he answered. "You gotta commit to findin' out; you gotta buy a ticket, and take the ride."

"'Less you gotta map," replied Ed'ard, chewing a mouthful

of buttermilk biscuit. Ed'ard had saved his biscuit in his coat pocket for later because he'd lost his appetite back at the café.

"That's cheating," quipped CD, "and you got some mustard on your tie."

Joe leaned forward to see around Ed'ard and looked at CD. "You talkin' about trains or marriage," he asked, inciting all three to laughter.

As Ed'ard worked on his mustard-stained tie with a handkerchief, they heard a whistle blow from a ways off signaling that the train to Charlottesville was coming into the station. They got up, collected their bags, which were stacked against the station wall, and stepped far enough away to allow the elderly and the women and children to board first.

When the train approached the platform, it pulled into the station far enough to ensure that all the passenger cars could be accessed. As the train's locomotive crept passed the end of the platform, CD noticed how dramatically it pushed the tracks into the ground.

"Great day in the morning," he exclaimed. "Did y'all see how far that thing mashed down the ground?"

"One thing's for sure," replied Joe, "You don't ever want to get under a train!"

CD laughed and shook his head in disbelief, "I reckon they don't make 'em out of feathers do they?"

Joe, Ed'ard, and CD boarded the train and found seats all together. Sitting down they took off their jackets.

While the porter was busy seeing that everyone's luggage was stowed, the train's whistle sounded one good long blast. Then the conductor began his walk from the front of the train to the caboose and then back again, all the while shouting, "All aboard!"

As the conductor began to step up onto the train, two strapping teenage boys ran across the platform toward him and stopped. They handed the conductor a half dollar each. He put the coins in his pocket and motioned for the boys to get onto the train.

"Those boys look to be twins," remarked Joe. "I bet they're goin' to the same place as us."

The train lurched forward, beginning the second and final leg of their journey to Charlottesville.

About halfway, the train passed through the tunnel under Afton Mountain. The entire train went dark, several passengers gasped, and somewhere in the front of the car, a child began to cry.

"I know exactly how he feels," said Ed'ard.

"Maybe some cold ox tongue would sooth your worry," laughed Joe.

Ed'ard kicked at Joe's feet in the darkness.

It wasn't long before all three had their jackets folded behind their heads and closed their eyes. Sleeping on a train is often easy. The rocking of the cars, as they glide along the rails, is like medicine. It coaxes a good, peaceful sleep.

Joe, Ed'ard, and CD woke from their napping to the sound of the train blowing its whistle as it pulled into the station in Charlottesville. They each craned to see out of the windows at the bustling town. CD was mesmerized. He looked this way and that, all up and down the boardwalk.

"There must be a thousand people in this town!" CD exclaimed.

Joe laughed and punched him in the shoulder, "A thousand wouldn't even come close.!"

"This is Charlottesville, Virginia, boy," said Ed'ard. "This is the place where Jefferson lived."

CD did not respond; he was busy taking in the sights. There were finely dressed people all over the platform waiting for loved ones to arrive or depart. There were vendors selling cigarettes and flowers, children playing games, and the lawmen were all wearing pistols.

Stepping down from the train, the Malone brothers noticed a crowd of men listening to a gentleman in a fancy suit, who was also handing out forms and pencils. There was a sign posted beside the man that read, "C&O Coal Recovery ".

"This must be where we sign up," said Joe.

All three brothers got in the line of men. After about 20 minutes of watching men leave the line with a form and then return it with all the information filled in, they had heard enough to know what to do.

By the time Joe got to the front of the line, the man had only two forms left. He gave one to Joe and the other to Ed'ard, then stepped back, and shouted, "Okay boys, we're all full. Sorry. If you hang around a few days, somebody might quit and you can try to take their spot."

"Sir! Sir!" shouted Ed'ard. "We come on the train, all the way from Paige County and you've hired me and one of my brothers, but CD here is our brother too, and he needs work, same as us."

"Sorry mister. All the spots are taken," replied the man.

CD stepped around Ed'ard and held up two hands pleading for him to stop and hear him out. The man sighed with an exasperated look on his face.

"Mister, I can do other work. I can do anything... I can even cook if I have to," said CD.

"Yeah, he knows how to burn all kinds of food," said Joe.

CD shot Joe a look and gritting his teeth mumbled, "You are not helping."

The railroad man reached inside the pocket of his jacket and produced a small piece of paper with a list on it.

"Only thing we need now are riggers," replied the man.

"I can do that," said CD.

The railroad man took off his hat and rubbed the back of his head, "It's real dangerous work, but it pays 25 cents a day more. I have one spot left if you want it."

"I'll take it!" said CD hurriedly.

"Alright," replied the man, "I can put you boys to work tomorrow morning... six o'clock sharp."

The railroad man walked into the station house and disappeared. The two other fellows, who were with him, stayed behind collecting the rest of the forms and then explained to the group the particulars of where they were staying and how they would draw their pay when the job was over.

Joe turned to CD, "Do you even know what a rigger is?"

"I have an idea," he replied. "Somebody who rigs up things, I reckon."

After an hour or so, ten surplus "Bulldog" trucks arrived at the station. They were outfitted with benches in the back so that each truck would hold around 12 men.

Joe, Ed'ard, and CD climbed up onto one of the trucks and sat down. The ride out to the work site was bumpy and rough. Most of the men kept silent as they were with strangers, but CD instantly struck up a conversation with the man next to him.

Putting out his hand he said, "CD Malone's my name. Pardon me for not standing."

The man shook his hand and told him his name. "I'm Henry Garrett," he replied. "You from around here?"

"No, we're all brothers. We come from Paige County," he answered, pointing at Joe and Ed'ard.

The man nodded a silent greeting.

"I'm Joe," "And I'm Edward," replied the brothers.

"I don't know where Paige County is," Henry replied.

Joe leaned around Ed'ard and CD, "It's just west of the Blue Ridge."

"You hillbillies come all this way just to shovel a little coal?" asked Henry with a bit of surprise in his tone.

CD frowned, "Where'd you come from?"

"Right over yonder," replied Henry pointing to a hill in the distance.

"I ain't gonna be shovelin' coal anyway. They got me signed up as a rigger," said CD.

"Me and Joe got the last two spots for shovelin' up the coal.

We thought we were gonna have to send our brother here... right back home on the train," Ed'ard said, patting CD on the knee.

CD pushed his hand away and grinning replied, "I've come here to work. I'm gonna get me enough money for a horse and to buy my wife a brand new Sunday dress."

"Say you're gonna be a rigger?" asked the man. "I hear that job is dangerous and only the colored hands will do it."

Put off by the man's rude manner, CD shot back, "Well, it pays two bits more a day!"

"That's to pay for your funeral," quipped Henry.

Ed'ard glanced at Joe with a worried look, but Joe shrugged it off.

CD sat back against the seat and stared straight ahead. He didn't speak the rest of the ride to the man camp.

Chapter 13

Trust

As they turned down the path to the "man camp", the truck that the Malone brothers were riding on stopped abruptly. There were two trucks stuck in the mud, and men and mules were pulling to get them out and going again.

Since the trucks were already stopped, the men took the opportunity to get down and stretch their legs. CD noticed that the last truck in the convoy was populated entirely by black men. He wondered if what this fellow, Henry, had said was true. He studied the men. They were laughing and talking and some were smoking cigarettes. They seemed no different than any other men he'd met, except for one. One of the men in the group was a head taller and noticeably bigger than the others. He looked like a prizefighter.

CD left the boys he was standing with and walked over to the men on the last truck. They all stopped and stared as he approached. CD loved meeting new people and he'd never met a stranger. He wore a smile on his face, oblivious to the idea that anyone might not instantly like him.

"I'm CD Malone," he shouted as he approached. "Are y'all riggers?"

The men all looked around at each other and laughed incredulously.

A short slim man stepped forward to speak for the group. He had a thin necktie and a mustache to match. He wore a grey tweed flat cap and black wool suit. He was dressed like a banker.

"What was that, what'd you say?" asked the man.

When CD was within arm's reach, he shook the man's hand, "I said... I'm CD Malone."

As the well-dressed man shook CD's hand, he glanced back at the others and gave a curious grin as if to say, "Do you believe this guy?"

"Somebody said you fellows are signed up to be riggers. That's what I signed up for too," said CD.

The man held onto CD's hand and said, "My name is Dr. Kevin Oden. Yes, we are here to help recover the derailed coal cars. You, um.... so far you are the only white boy assigned to our crew."

CD withdrew his hand, "Is that a problem?"

Dr. Oden walked over and stood next to the exceptionally large man in their group. "Only if you make it one," he replied with a smile.

It was instantly clear to CD that his acceptance by the black workers would require some effort. Still, he wanted the money, and even more than the money, he wanted to see the look on Leola's face when he gave her a fancy, new store-bought dress. He wasn't going to let anything deter him.

Walking back over toward Joe and Ed'ard, CD noticed that all the boys from his truck were staring at him. He felt uncomfortable and set his jaw in anticipation of what they might say.

"So, is that who you'll be workin' with?" asked Ed'ard.

CD turned and looked back at the other riggers and replied, "Yep. That one fella looks strong as an ox and the man in the black suit and cap says he's a doctor."

"Ain't no such thing as a colored doctor!" shouted Henry Garrett with indignation.

Suddenly, one of the railroad men called out, "Okay, you boys load up."

The Malone brothers climbed back up onto the truck. CD worked to maneuver to a seat up closer to the cab so that the rude fellow, Henry, couldn't sit next to him. The truck began to move again and CD tried not to think about what the extra twenty-five cents might be for.

When the trucks finally arrived and came to a stop, all the men got down and were directed to different sections of the small four-man tents.

The railroad had set a man camp near the site of the derailed coal cars. The tents were set up on thin wooden platforms in a grid. There were a few bathhouses and one tent for the chow hall. There was another smaller man camp set up some distance from the main camp.

Pointing at the large tent Joe remarked, "I bet you could hold a three-ring circus in there."

"You men," shouted a man pointing at the Malone boys, "If you don't want to sleep out in the rain, follow me."

Walking behind the man, Joe glanced back at his two brothers and raised his eyebrows.

"Everybody here is so uncouth," whispered CD.

Ed'ard replied, "I think they're just in a hurry."

Arriving at their tents, they dropped their bags and sat down to check out the canvas cots the railroad had provided. On each cot was a pair of wool Army surplus blankets folded at one end.

Ed'ard patted the blanket and sighed.

"What?" asked CD.

Ed'ard laughed and said, "I've slept under these Army blankets before. But hopefully, nobody will be throwing artillery at me this time."

The brothers sat and chatted for a while until the crew chief announced that supper would be at six o'clock sharp, in the mess tent. He explained that after everyone ate, they would be divided into work crews and be given tools.

At a quarter to six, Joe got up off his cot and put on his jacket. Ed'ard and CD were still napping, so he stirred them awake and said, "C'mon boys, we best head over to the big tent."

CD and Ed'ard sat up and put their boots on. Donning their jackets, they followed Joe to the mess tent. When they got to the tent, there was already a line of men waiting to be let in.

"We're early," complained Ed'ard.

CD poked him on the shoulder and replied, "Remember what daddy taught us. Better to be an hour early than a minute late."

After a few minutes, the mess tent was opened and the line of men began to move inside. When the brothers finally reached the serving line, CD turned to his brothers and said, "Looks like we're having a turkey dinner."

They passed each station and watched as servers piled their trays with mashed potatoes, gravy, green beans, a healthy slice of turkey meat, and a roll.

Ed'ard looked at the feast the railroad had provided and remarked that it was more food than he had ever seen in one place since he got out of the Army.

Once everyone had finished eating, a man with the railroad got up on a platform with a public address apparatus set up in front of it. He was a big burly man with a full beard that hung all the way down to his chest. He walked up to the microphone and began to speak. The microphone made a terrible, loud squeal. Some of the men covered their ears and groaned.

In a hurry, another fellow ran over and adjusted some controls in front of the stage and then the railroad man continued, "I'm Donald Fountain, I work for the C&O Railroad. The Railroad has put me in charge of this operation, we have a whole team of experienced men leading the recovery of the derailed train cars. Meanwhile, you men have been brought here as the muscle, to salvage as much coal as we can."

Mr. Fountain made it clear that the men hired to clean up after the derailment were not to think of themselves as the brains, only as the brawn, and that the Railroad was more concerned with recovering the coal cars than the actual coal.

"Good Appalachian coal is certainly valuable, but the real worth is in the derailed cars. Our main objective is to restore those cars to the tracks, so they can be repaired and put back into service. The great Chesapeake and Ohio is counting on *you* to get it done," he explained.

Joe whispered across the table to Ed'ard and CD, "Looks like we didn't need to bring our smarts... just our backs."

CD and Ed'ard each gave a sarcastic grin and listened as the man finished his speech. He informed them that everyone would be assigned to work crews based on the information they'd filled out on their hiring forms.

The next morning, all the men reported to the mess tent at five-thirty AM and ate a hearty breakfast of flapjacks, maple syrup, eggs, and ham. There was coffee and milk in large pots, and a man standing behind each pot with a ladle serving it up.

CD, Ed'ard, and Joe got their food and sat down at one of the tables. The tables were crudely made from wooden planks and along each side were simple wooden benches with no backrests.

"Man alive," said Ed'ard, "These boys cook almost as good as mama."

Joe nodded in agreement, shifted his mouthful of food into his cheek, and mumbled, "Don't let her hear you say that."

When breakfast was over, the men were led out to the site of the derailment.

Over a dozen high-side gondolas were lying beside the tracks. The cars were facing this way and that. Some were right side up and some were upside down. Coal was everywhere. A few of the cars, that were still upright, were full of coal and had to be emptied of their weighty cargo before they could be lifted and placed back on the tracks. Cleaning up the derailment would be a herculean task.

Seeing the sight for the first time, Ed'ard was stunned, he stopped walking and remarked, "There ain't no way—a *thousand* men couldn't clean all that up!"

"Well, I don't care either way," said a man standing next to the Malone brothers, "As long as they pay me, that's all I care about."

One of the C&O men walked pasted Ed'ard as he made his remarks and replied, "Best way to eat an elephant is one bite at a time. Easy as cake!"

Walking on, they saw foremen waiting for the hired men to arrive. There was a man from the railroad passing out shovels while the supervisors gathered teams of men and led them to the different areas where they would be shoveling the coal into mule carts and trucks.

Ed'ard and Joe left with a small, loud, balding man who was shouting and pointing.

CD stood and looked around. He didn't see any of the men he'd met the day before.

Suddenly, a tall thin man, who was missing an arm, hollered at him, "You there, where are you supposed to be?"

CD walked over to the man and put out his hand to shake, but withdrew it as soon as he realized the man was missing his right arm. He felt surprised and embarrassed at what he'd done.

The man saw the regret on CD's face and laughed, "Son, the last thing I shook hands with was a German artillery shell. It's okay. Saves me the trouble."

The railroad man asked CD which crew he'd been assigned to. CD told him that he was a rigger, the man pointed and said, "Over there."

Far off, at the end of the worksite, CD could see a large steam crane on the railroad tracks and a group of black men already working.

As CD walked the distance to reach the other riggers, he marveled at the sheer number of men working and how much coal they would have to move. When CD finally got over to the area where the other riggers were working, the crane was in place and the steel cables were shackled to the rail car so it could be pulled upright.

The fellow with the thin mustache, Dr. Oden, walked over and looked CD up and down. "Well, well, well, we all took bets on whether you'd show up," said Dr. Oden.

He looked over his shoulder and shouted toward the others, "Hey, Jerome, you owe me a dime!" Turning back to look at CD, he grinned, "Come with me."

CD followed him over to the railcar they were working on. The exceptionally large man just stood, staring at him. So, CD (as he usually did) stuck out his hand and stated his name. "My name is Charles Daniel Malone, folks just call me CD," he said.

The giant man did not shake his hand but instead put a shovel in it and replied, "I'm Jerome Braswell... people call me *Sir.*"

"Okay, well good to meet you, Sir," replied CD.

Out of earshot of CD, two of the other men who were busy shoveling coal, so they could crawl under an overturned railcar, remarked to one another about CD either being the friendliest man they had ever met or the stupidest.

The riggers worked all day and managed to get two of the rail cars back on the tracks.

By the time the day was through, CD and all the other men, for that matter, were spent. They were all dirty, sweaty, and hungry. When quitting time came, every crew began the short migration back to the man camp.

All the way back, CD pestered the other men with questions about where they came from and about their families. He told them about his two brothers and all about his family back home in Paige County.

"You sure do talk a lot, don't you?" said one man, visibly annoyed. "I bet you could talk the ears off a cornfield."

Dr. Oden called out from the rear of the group, "He's a hillbilly, he's not accustomed to being in the company of..." he paused for effect and then continued, "such fine human specimens." All the men laughed.

CD wanted to laugh, but he wasn't sure if he'd earned his place with the other men yet.

When they reached the camp, CD parted from the group

and headed back over to the tent he shared with Joe and Ed'ard. They were already back and cleaned up for supper.

"Better hurry and wash up," said Joe, "supper's at seven sharp."

After supper, the Malone brothers laid down on their cots to sleep.

Lying there in the fading moments of the evening light, Ed'ard's curiosity was overpowering.

"So what were they like?" he asked.

CD thought a minute, he knew what he was asking, and replied, "Well, they're just like any other men, I guess, except they sing a lot while they work."

Joe spoke up, "I reckon some of the other boys here don't like you working with 'em. They don't think it's right."

"Earnin' my pay and takin' care of my family is what's right!" CD barked.

"Don't get mad at us," said Ed'ard, "we don't care either way."

"Yeah, I know. I'm sorry," replied CD. "It was a hard day and I'm just tired. Besides the other fellas on the crew don't like me... or maybe it's that they don't trust me."

Ed'ard offered some consolation that maybe the other men on the rigging crew just needed to get to know him a little first, and then surely they'd see what a good man he was.

Ed'ard and CD were getting nowhere, working out the intricacies of trust and friendship in their half-asleep fatigue. As entertaining as it was to Joe, it occurred to him that perhaps there was a deeper issue.

"*Trust* and *like* are way different. You can trust someone you don't like and like someone you don't trust," said Joe. "I like my number-two mule, but I can't trust him, and I trust a rattlesnake to always do what rattlers do, but I sure don't like him."

"That makes a lot of sense, I guess," replied CD, "Maybe I should work on gettin' them to trust me, and then if they like me, that's just extra butter on the biscuit."

"I think you just concentrate on bein' respectful, mindin' your manners, and carryin' your family name well," offered Ed'ard.

"Y'all remember that horse daddy got for free from Mr. Coe?" asked Joe.

CD laughing replied, "Yep, I remember when it threw you over a three-rail fence!"

"Right," said Joe, "Turns out the reason Mr. Coe got him for free, and gave him to us, is because that horse had been mistreated, mistreated for so long that he didn't trust people anymore."

There was a long silence, and the wisdom of Joe's insight sank into the deep places of CD's heart.

"Well, I'll show 'em, the Malone boys ain't got a mean bone in their bodies," said CD.

"Alright, enough jawin', tomorrow's another hard day. See you boys in the morning," said Joe.

CD and Ed'ard replied with, "Good night," and all three fell asleep.

Hard physical labor is responsible for more hours of good,

sound sleep than is anything else. There's no mystery to it. The human body is an incredible machine, and when we invest in it a day of hard work, it rewards us with blissful slumber. The Malone brothers slept that night, just the same as they always had... hard work was nothing new to them, and it fit them as well as their own shoes.

Chapter 14

Not Welcomed Here

At five o'clock in the morning, a train whistle blew to awaken the sleeping men at the camp. Joe sat up first and looked around startled and barked, "For cryin' out loud!"

CD and Ed'ard stirred and when the whistled sounded again, they both sat up. Ed'ard stretched his arms over his head let out a long groan.

After putting his shoes on, CD picked up his towel and toothbrush and said, "Well, I'm gonna go brush my teeth and wash this sleep off my face before the bathhouse gets crowded. I liked to never got in there yesterday."

Joe laughed and replied, "Well, I don't care if you boys brush your teeth in the mornings as long as you wash up in the evenings. I ain't sharin' my tent with smelly folk!"

"Your tent?" replied Ed'ard.

"I reckon every part I can smell is mine," came Joe's response.

Ed'ard made a raspberry at Joe and shoved his cot with his foot.

When the chow hall bell rang, most of the men were already waiting in line to get their breakfast. The serving line moved quickly. Everything on the menu was served from enormous pots with large spoons.

CD turned to look at Ed'ard and Joe, "Looks like these boys have slopped a few hogs in their day."

As he went through the line, CD spoke to every single person who was serving up the food. There were scrambled eggs, grits, hashed potatoes, biscuits with red-eye gravy, and oatmeal with raisins in it.

Joe made a remark about the raisins, "Looks like bugs got in that oatmeal."

Ed'ard was behind him in line, as the man dishing out the oatmeal put his serving spoon in the pot, Ed'ard politely declined.

"What's the matter Ed'ard, rather have some cold ox tongue?" laughed CD.

Ed'ard did not acknowledge his brother and just kept walking down the chow line over to the coffee service.

The three brothers found a spot at one of the long tables and sat down. CD got up to go find salt and pepper shakers and get a cup of joe. As he walked over to the service table, he could see out of the opening in their mess tent over to the smaller one that had been set up for the black workers.

He looked inside. Although it was too far away to make out faces, he recognized Jerome. He was easy to spot because he was so much taller than any other man. From inside their mess tent, CD could hear piano music and singing. He smiled and picked up the salt and pepper shakers. Returning to the table, he found Joe and Ed'ard with empty trays.

"You boys finished already?" he asked.

"We couldn't wait on dawdlin' service," quipped Ed'ard, "We're what you call, workin' men."

"You were gone a while, I reckon yours is probably cold," added Joe.

CD looked at his tray. Steam was no longer rising from his grits. "Cold or not, I'll eat it, every bite," he said. He sat down, shook a good measure of salt over his tray, and scooped a spoon full of thickened grits. When his mouth was full, he looked for his coffee and remembered he'd forgotten it.

"Forgot my coffee," he mumbled.

"I'll get you a cup," said Joe.

Joe got up and walked over to the coffee service where a short stout man was handing out coffee and milk.

"What'll it be," asked the man.

"My brother forgot his coffee," said Joe pointing in the direction of CD.

"Your brother is that hillbilly workin' with them colored boys," said the man disapprovingly. "How does he take his coffee? Let me guess...black!" The small man smiled a self-satisfied grin and put the cup of coffee down on the table.

Joe picked up the cup, and considered saying something to the man, but thought better of it. He decided that the rude fellow was not worth the trouble it would cause to pursue the matter.

Ed'ard and CD could see it was taking longer than it should

for the man to give Joe the coffee. They looked at each other and Ed'ard shrugged his shoulders.

When Joe returned with the cup of coffee, he set it down in front of CD and took his seat. He didn't speak but smirked shaking his head.

"Everything okay?" asked CD.

"The *little* fellow fancies himself a funnyman," he replied.

At seven o'clock, the day's work began with much commotion, as over a hundred and fifty men and all the equipment needed to continue the job of cleaning up the coal and recovering the train cars began their laborious tasks. There were big trucks sloshing their way back and forth, teams of mules and horses pulling carts and wagons, and men shoveling coal. They were shoveling tons and tons of coal.

As CD began the long march out to his worksite, he could see that the other men from his crew were already a good ways ahead of him. He decided to run to catch up. When CD was just a few feet behind the group, he slowed to a walking pace.

Dr. Oden, hearing the sound of CD's footsteps, looked over his shoulder. "Well, good morning Hillbilly," greeted Dr. Oden. "I hope you slept well and ate a hearty breakfast because today the real work begins."

"Hard work is hard work, I guess," replied a breathless CD.

"What did you say your name was again, Hillbilly?" he asked.

"Charles Daniel Malone, but people call me CD," he answered.

"Uh huh," grunted Dr. Oden. "Hillbilly it is."

"Well, what'll I call you?" asked CD. "I don't figure I'll have breath to spare, to say Dr. Oden all day long. So, how about Doc?"

Dr. Oden stopped walking. He looked at CD with surprise... almost respect.

When the two of them caught up to the rest of the group, they got right to work. The day went on like any other, and the men managed to recover three more rail cars. Over the course of the day, the men successfully restored two coal cars to the tracks and placed one on a flatbed car to be scrapped.

As the day wore on, CD became more and more fascinated by the way the men on the crew laughed, joked, and sang. There was a rhythm to the way they interacted with each other. There was balance and immense respect in the way disagreements got settled and decisions were made.

A spirit of cooperation seemed to guide every move. These men also worked exceptionally hard and took very few breaks. CD noticed the easy way these men, who were strangers just days before, seemed to be around each other, as well as how easily and naturally they seemed to distrust him.

During one of their breaks, Jerome stood by the water barrel. As the line of men passed the barrel, he filled each of their cups. As CD approached, Jerome dipped the ladle and held it in his hand. Looking directly at CD, he took a sip of water from the ladle and threw the rest out on the ground. He hung the ladle back on the side of the barrel and then walked away. He stopped to rest in the shade of a willow oak that was just beginning to regrow its leaves.

Stunned, CD thought for a minute, *What'd he do that for? Was the big man picking a fight?* It seemed unlikely that he would pick a fight with a man half his size.

Deciding that it was a test, and also being rather parched, CD picked up the ladle and filled his cup. Never breaking eye contact with Jerome, he turned up the cup and drank it dry. He reached for the ladle and refilled his cup. Before CD could get the cup to his lips, for a second time, the other men from the crew erupted in laughter and cheers.

One of the men came over to refill his cup and holding it aloft yelled, "A toast, to the Hillbilly!"

"Hillbilly!" shouted the men in unison.

CD grinned. His grin gave way to a nervous smile and then to laughter. By the end of that day, CD had learned a few songs, a few things about the other men, and a great many things about himself.

After supper, he regaled his two brothers with stories from the day's work. He shared jokes with them that the other men on his crew had taught him, and he told them all about how most of the men seemed to be church-going folk.

"These fellas don't swear and they never take the Lord's name in vain. Why, Doc even leads us in a prayer each day before we start to work," said CD.

"Doc?" asked Ed'ard.

CD sat up on his bunk, "He's the fellow with the pencil mustache. He's a doctor of some sort. Not a real doctor or anything, one of them that teaches at a college. You know...like a professor."

"A man has to be real smart, to get that far in school," said Joe, "Even smarter if he's colored, I expect."

"He's a hard man to understand, but it sure is something to hear him talk," mused CD.

Ed'ard rolled over on his bunk to look at CD, "What do you mean?"

"I don't know. I guess he talks kind of fancy, but not to make everyone else feel dumb. It's more like he thinks we're as smart as he is," replied CD.

"Keep your distance boy," chuckled Joe, "If he gets to know you, he'll be in for a real let-down."

Joe and Ed'ard laughed while CD reached a hand over to try to steal Joe's blanket. He tugged on it, but Joe's grip was firm.

The three brothers said "goodnight" and went off to sleep. The night passed quickly but left enough time for CD to dream. In the dream, he was falling. Like many people, CD occasionally dreamed he was flying or falling or doing some other strange thing only permitted in dreams. Of the few other times CD had dreamed he was falling, he was always falling off a cliff or a high rock in broad daylight, but this time was different. This time he dreamed he was falling into darkness... total and complete darkness.

The following morning at 5:00 AM the steam whistle sounded again.

Joe was startled awake so violently that he rolled off his cot onto the wooden platform. "Dagblast it! I swear I'm gonna smash that confounded horn with a hammer!" he yelled.

Joe's shouting woke CD, but Ed'ard was already awake, lying in his bunk. He'd awakened on his own, just a few minutes before the whistle blew, and watching his pocket watch, kept an eye on Joe. Of the five children that Warner and Mary Ethel had, Joe was the jumpiest. Ever since he was a boy, his brothers and sisters would entertain themselves by hiding behind a door or a haystack so they could jump out and scare Joe.

Remembering how the whistle had startled Joe so violently the day before, Ed'ard was pleased that he had awakened in time to see it for himself.

As Joe got up off the floor, he saw Ed'ard lying there in his cot laughing as quietly as he could. CD was awake by this time too and inquired as to why Joe was crawling around on the floor.

"Did you lose your ox tongue?" asked CD.

"You're *not* a funnyman Charles Daniel," snorted Joe.

Still laughing, Ed'ard managed to squeak, "Who needs a funnyman when we got you?"

Joe kicked at Ed'ard's cot and ordered him and CD out of bed.

At breakfast, the three brothers got their food and found an empty spot at one of the long tables. Before CD could set his tray of food down, a man seated next to him put his hand on the table in the way.

"I think you're in the wrong mess tent, boy," said the man. "Your kind is out yonder." He pointed towards the smaller chow hall set up for the black workers.

Joe and Ed'ard jumped to their feet. Instantly, a couple of dozen other men got up—Joe, Ed'ard, and CD were greatly outnumbered. It was clear to CD that if this situation escalated, at all, it would mean the end of their financial opportunity and maybe even the end of them.

"Sir, you're uncouth," said CD, "but maybe you're right, maybe that is my mess hall."

As CD picked up his tray to leave, the only noise was the sound of CD's footsteps as he walked out of the tent. Disgusted, Joe and Ed'ard picked up their trays and moved to the end of another table that was empty and far from anyone else.

The men who had stood up against the Malones sat back down, and the bully who'd sent CD out of the mess hall said, "Can you believe he called me that? What's uncouth mean anyway?" Several of the other men laughed.

Walking from the main chow hall, CD decided that if he were not welcomed in the other tent, he'd find himself a stump to sit on. He figured it would be better to eat alone than with rude, mean, ignorant folk.

He stepped through the opening of the smaller mess tent and once again, the place fell silent. Every man in the chow hall turned to look at him.

One of the men walked over from the coffee service to CD, and smiling asked, "You get lost, Hillbilly?"

"No, I just figured I should take my meals with my own crew is all," he replied.

The man looked over CD's shoulder. He could see a handful of men from the white mess hall staring from the doorway. Piecing together what had taken place, he put a hand on CD's shoulder and led him to an empty place at one of the tables.

"Hillbilly's gonna eat with us, if that's okay," announced the man.

A few of the men were unsure, but before anyone could object, Jerome stood up and pulled an empty chair out for CD at his table, and with a booming voice said, "That'll be just fine."

CD sat down and tore into his food as if he was half starved. Part it was nerves and part of it was anger... good and righteous anger.

Seated at the same table as Jerome, Dr. Oden watched as CD devoured his food without speaking. He looked at the other men at the table with a familiar sadness and lowered his head, as one might if he was praying.

"Is that the first time you been thrown out?" asked one of the men.

Dr. Oden looked up and took off his glasses, "Feels different when it's you, doesn't it?" He paused and pointed his finger around the room, "Every man in this room knows what you're feeling right now, Hillbilly."

CD stopped eating and put down his fork. He put his elbows on the table, clasped his hands, and rested his chin. He was so angry he could hardly contain it. He wore it all over his face.

"It's called egocentrism," said Doc.

"Ego what?" asked Jerome.

Doc smiled, "Egocentrism. It means that if all you ever know is yourself and your own kind, you sort of think everything in the world is either about you or for you. That kind of thinking leaves no space for anyone that isn't like yourself."

"I just want to go back in there and cave in that fellow's skull," said CD softly. He was half-shocked that such a thing had come out of his mouth, but he meant it—more than that, *he felt it.*

"Why?" asked Dr. Oden thoughtfully, "For us... or for you?"

CD did not reply. He'd said enough already... maybe too much.

The whistle sounded, alerting all the crews to begin reporting to their work areas. Picking up his tray, CD stood up from the table. His food was half-eaten and now cold. He put a biscuit in his pocket and placed the tray on the dirty-crockery table.

The march out to the worksite was quiet for CD. He hung back, keeping a short distance between himself and the other men. He struggled to make sense of what happened and the question Doc had asked. He wondered if he was angry because of the man's bigotry toward the other members of his crew or because it had come so close to himself.

Jerome was in the middle of the group and looking back, noticed CD walking alone. He slowed his pace until he was side by side with CD. The two men walked together for a spell without speaking. CD was staring straight ahead, still boiling with a range of emotions... pain, anger, regret, and worry. Jerome walked quietly with him and tried to think of something to say. Nothing seemed simple enough for the short time they had left before they reached the worksite.

"I got a preacher back home," Jerome began, "that tells me we are all God's children, we are all made in his image, and he loves us... every one! Sometimes, when I look in the mirror, I don't see it. I see a man that has made many mistakes and I wonder, 'How could a righteous God love a sinner like me'?"

"That man, that made you leave the mess hall, is just like me... only difference... is maybe he don't know it yet. Maybe, one day, he'll look in the mirror and wonder if God loves *him* too."

"I don't think I've ever felt so much hate all at once. It made me sick to my stomach that I could feel that way," replied CD.

Jerome was sorry this thing had happened to his new friend; he had felt that same hate in himself, many times. He stopped walking and quietly said, "Hillbilly," there was a brotherly tone in Jerome's voice, like Joe used, when he had something important to tell him. CD stopped walking and stared at the ground. Jerome continued, "Hatred only grows if you feed it. Don't let what that man sowed today take root."

Chapter 15

The Third Car

Moving heavy objects is demanding. Moving coal cars that weigh forty thousand pounds is *exceptionally* demanding. The railroad foreman had slated three gondolas for recovery that day. One of the cars was clear of any debris, but two of the cars had come to rest tangled, one atop the other. Another steam crane had to be brought to the site to aid in the effort. The additional crane would enable the recovery crew to secure one car while they restored the other to the tracks.

Each day started with prayer and Dr. Oden was the person the men trusted to lead them. They assembled and removed their hats. Some of the men bowed their heads, some closed their eyes, and some... *some* raised their hands toward heaven with their eyes looking up.

Doc stepped into the center of the group and began, "Lord, today we take up the monumental task of moving these rail cars. We ask for safety, wisdom, and patience. And Lord, today we are especially grateful for the way you show us your grace," he paused, raised his head, and made eye contact with CD, "even when it comes to us as righteous indignation. Amen."

When he had finished the prayer, he walked past CD and patted him once on the shoulder.

The gesture was nearly more than CD could accept and still maintain his composure.

All morning, the crew worked to jack up and place cribbing under the two tangled gondolas. They were waiting for the steam crane operators to get both cranes into position. Making use of every minute, the crew decided to get a head start preparing the third car so that when the two tangled cars were recovered, the work of getting it on the tracks would be that much further along.

Teams of men with long metal bars, shovels, and jacks worked around the overturned coal car. Inch by inch, they raised the car with hydraulic jacks and then shored it up with large wooden beams stacked like log cabins. Once it was secured properly, it left the train car raised on the downhill side almost four feet off the ground, while the uphill side of the coal car was still partially buried in the muddy hillside

When they had finished the preparations on the single car, the men took a break. CD was closest to the water barrel when the foreman called out, "Break time!"

He seized the opportunity to serve his teammates and made the effort to be first to the water barrel. He picked up the ladle and happily supplied each man with as much water as they required. More and more, as the men passed through the line to receive the water, CD began to relax. He felt a good happiness that eclipsed the events from the chow hall that morning. When everyone had gotten their water, the men spent the remaining few minutes chatting about this and that.

"How many young'uns you got?" asked Jerome.

"Just one," he replied. "What about you, Jerome, you got family?"

"Yes, sir," he replied, "I got a wife and two boys. They're as fine as any man could ask for. I got a nine-year-old named Thomas and a twelve-year-old named Jerome Jr."

CD smiled, "My boy is gonna be twelve in November."

"My wife says she prefers cold weather babies because it's easier to warm a house in winter than to cool it in summer. Was your boy born at home like mine?" asked Jerome.

"Naw," replied CD, "We adopted our boy. My daddy and little brother found him wanderin' on the road in the rain when he was about four."

Jerome looked puzzled. "Then how do you know he'll be twelve in November?" he asked.

"Well, we don't," said CD, "When he finally started to talk, he said he was four, so we just celebrate his birthday on the day we found him."

The big man shook his head in disbelief. "Must be some mighty fine people where you come from," he paused, "to take in a stray like that."

"My wife, Leola, says he was sent to us. The Sheriff called around for weeks and couldn't find his folks. So *we* gave him a home," he explained.

Jerome smiled and asked, "What's his name?"

"We call him Pink," he answered.

Everyone within earshot stopped and looked at CD. They all had a curious, if not shocked, look on their faces.

"Did *you* name him that or was that his name already? Or is that some sort of family name?" asked Jerome. It was clear that he could not understand why anyone would name a boy, "Pink."

CD laughed, "Well, that ain't his real name, but it's the only word he said for several days after we found him, so it stuck. Everybody calls him that. He don't seem to mind at all."

"Okay," shouted the railroad foreman, "Let's get back after it!"

Dr. Oden drank down the last of his water, put the cup on the table beside the barrel, and looking at CD, said, "The world is full of men with fine-sounding names who haven't good character. If your son, Pink, turns out like his father, then I contend, it is a virtual certainty his name will be spoken with respect. The character of a man makes the name—not the other way around."

Doc's words made CD's heart swell.

"Get this cable down on the underside of that car and shackle it to the axle," shouted the railroad foreman.

CD and three others dragged the cable the fifty or so feet to the end of the coal car. Spring rains had fallen almost every evening making the slopes near the tracks slippery. Struggling for good footing, the men slipped and fell in a heap. CD landed at the bottom of the pile and when he emerged, he was covered in mud. It was even in his mouth.

One of the men reached out a hand to help him up and straining remarked, "Hillbilly, you have to be the happiest man I ever met."

"Huh," CD grunted.

Laughing, the man replied, "You're the only fellow I ever met who smiles while he's fallin' face first in the mud."

CD and the other men laughed. His mind drifted back to a conversation he'd had with an older gentleman at church—after he'd been teased a bit. "Givin' you a hard time is how you know we like you," the man explained. He hoped that the men laughing at his muddy smile meant that they really did like him.

Once the hook was secured to the overturned rail car, the crane operator began to reel in the cable. Under the power of the steam crane's winch, the railcar moved, but stubbornly. Separating the two tangled railcars was not easy. Some of the wooden slats on the sides of the cars had to be cut away and large pieces of steel dismantled. It was slow going, muddy, and difficult. The waterlogged terrain and the noise of the heavy machinery made it hard to move and hard to hear.

At noon, men from the railroad handed each of the riggers their lunch. CD and the other men found a place to sit and opened the brown paper sacks to find two ham biscuits, an apple, and a slice of lemon cake.

"Looky here," shouted one of the men holding up his slice of cake. "Lemon cake is my favorite!"

Jerome smiled at the man and reciprocated by holding up his own slice of cake.

CD opened the paper sack, unwrapped the lemon cake from the wax paper and scarfed it down. He wasn't sure Leola would have approved, but being far away from home, working so hard in the sun, and dealing with the difficulties he'd faced that morning, he decided he needed dessert first.

After the men ate, some talked and some tried to get a nap in the shade.

When the lunch hour concluded, work resumed to restore the two tangled cars to the tracks. There were several setbacks that afternoon and it began to look like the men would be lucky to have the two tangled cars back on the tracks by quitting time, let alone the third car scheduled for the day.

At a quarter to four, the second of the two tangled coal cars was rolling behind a tug on the railroad tracks. The men cheered and took a break to get some water.

All day long, as part of the recovery operation, cranes and switcher locomotives had traveled up and down the tracks where the men were working. Each time the heavy machines passed by, the earth beneath the tracks compressed noticeably.

This compression is normal and is accounted for in the design of the railroad bed, the crossties, and the tracks them-selves. However, this day was a little different, in that a twenty-ton gondola was lying on its side, shored up with timbers, waiting to be hoisted back onto the railroad tracks.

Unbeknownst to the rigging crew, each time a heavy machine passed the overturned coal car, its shoring timbers shifted a small amount in the waterlogged soil. One of the timbers in the back of the stack had broken, and all the others in the stack were now slowly sliding out from under the coal car. Each time the steam crane or switcher passed, the timbers slipped a little bit more.

While the men were getting a drink of water, the railroad foreman walked over to where Doc and a few of the riggers were standing and asked whether they thought the men could get the third car up on the tracks before quitting time. The other option was to finish the day preparing a different derailed gondola for rigging and recovery for the following workday.

In talking it over with the crew, Doc explained that once they began the operation they would likely have to see it through... even if it meant working late. Naturally, the men avoided working late because they were paid by the day, not the hour.

Deciding to stay on schedule and recover the third car, the men began to relocate. CD reached the third coal car first, he squatted down and held out his hand for the winch cable. A pair of the other men dragged the cable to him, and CD disappeared with it under the rail car.

From under the car, CD could hear the steam-powered locomotive and the number one crane throttling up. He wanted to hurry and rig the cable to the axle since it would speed things along if the cable was already set by the time everyone else was ready to right the overturned car.

Once under the coal car, he noticed that one of the timber cribs had sunk into the ground and shifted quite a bit. The immense weight of the car and the muddy soil had caused the stack of timbers to lean dramatically to one side. A couple of the timbers were broken and had fallen out of the stack. He sat for a minute wondering what to do, *"Should I keep going or go tell the foreman about this?"*

He decided to chance it and began to crawl further under the gondola when a voice inside said, *"Get out!"* He laughed, figuring it was probably his imagination getting the better of him. He inched forward and heard the voice say, *"Run!"* CD froze —trying to make up his mind.

On the one hand, he knew that any significant delays would mean the crew would fall behind, but on the other hand, he sure didn't want the coal car to fall on him. All at once, he felt a deep panic—he turned around and started to crawl out. In his hurry, CD brushed against a heavy steel cable that was frayed near the end. It caught his shirt, making it difficult to move. He struggled to free himself, but the steel strands that had penetrated his shirt would not let go.

"Hey!" CD yelled. "I'm coming out. Pull that cable out from under here. I'm caught in it!" But CD's cries were not heard, as there was far too much noise from the locomotive and the steam crane for anyone to hear.

Meanwhile, the railroad crews began moving the second crane and the switcher locomotive to a sidetrack. The boiler on the steam crane had gone out, so the pilot decided to push it to the sidetrack with the locomotive. As the two machines moved together past the third car, the added weight caused the already loosened timbers to give way.

Suddenly, one end of the coal car collapsed onto the ground with a deafening boom. The twenty-ton gondola splashed mud and rocks all over the workers who were standing by.

Everyone stood stunned. In vain, Jerome and a couple of others reflexively grabbed nearby timbers and tried shoving them under the car. The men called out for CD but heard no reply.

Under the coal car, CD had managed to roll over and pull himself a couple of feet closer to the opening—*when his entire world went dark.*

Someone shouted to the foreman, "There's a man under there!"

Immediately the switcher locomotive stopped and the pilot got out and ran down the hill to see what had happened. The railroad foreman barked for him to get back into the switcher and move the locomotive out of the way.

"Get that thing out of here!" he shouted. Then pointing at the crane operators, he added, "And get that boiler fired back up... now!"

A few men ran over to assist the crane operators in re-lighting the boiler on the second crane. Instinctively, the rest of the crew began to dig under the coal car to try and reach their trapped crewmate.

"Alright, alright," shouted the foreman. Signaling to the men who were not busy digging, "Everybody over here!" he yelled. He gathered the men together to begin planning how they would go about retrieving CD. The recovery job had now become a rescue operation.

By the time a plan of action was agreed upon; it was quitting time, the second steam crane's boiler had been fired back up, and more railroad men had arrived at the site. While the steam crane's firebox was fed wood and coal, the rest of the crew continued to dig. A group of men gathered more timbers to shore up the gondola, once it was ready to lift. Some of the men took off their shirts to use in place of buckets, filling them with dirt and rocks. Load after load, the men worked to tunnel their way to CD.

As word spread, more men arrived to help. After quitting time, almost every man on the site had come to see.

Joe and Ed'ard were walking back to camp, when they heard the commotion. They turned and saw most everyone heading down to the area where the riggers had been working. Deciding to go see what all the fuss was about, the pair made their way over to the crowd that had swelled to at least a hundred men.

When they reached the crowd, Joe asked one of the men what was going on.

"They say one of them coal cars collapsed and there's men trapped under it," he answered.

Joe and Ed'ard pushed their way through the crowd and tried to find CD. There was so much chaos and so many men that it was impossible.

A railroad man with a megaphone got up on the back of a bulldog truck and yelled, "You men head back to camp. Everything is under control here. If you are needed, someone will come and get you. Now get back to camp and rest up... work starts tomorrow at seven AM!"

Joe, Ed'ard, and the throng of men all turned and began the muddy slog back to the camp. There was a breeze blowing in their faces from the mess tent carrying the smell of fried chicken.

"CD better hurry up and get back here," said Ed'ard, "Fried chicken is his favorite."

Chapter 16

Leaning On the Everlasting Arms

E d'ard and Joe waited a while before going to supper. The bell had rung a half hour ago and Ed'ard was looking forward to the chicken he'd smelled earlier.

"I reckon we done waited long enough," he complained.

"Keep your shirt on, boy," replied Joe. In his gut, Joe felt something wasn't right.

"I'm just worried that all the short legs might be picked over by the time we get there," replied Ed'ard.

"Well, you might just be worried about the wrong thing. What if CD is one of the ones trapped under that railroad car," Joe shot back.

Ed'ard gestured toward the work site, "Oh, I bet CD's probably leading the charge to get them fellas out."

"Well, in any case we ought to pray for them," Joe suggested.

The two brothers sat back down on their cots and silently

prayed that all would be well for the other workers on CD's crew. After another few minutes, the brothers decided to go eat.

"We best go on and get a bite," said Joe, "If CD comes to fetch us, we won't be any help on an empty stomach."

"I hope they do come get us," said Ed'ard, "I want to meet them fellas he's been talkin' about."

"Yep," replied Joe, "Sounds like he's been having more fun at his job than we have at ours."

When they walked into the mess tent, they noticed about a dozen men in deep conversation at one of the nearby tables. Some were wearing work hats with carbide lights on them, while one gentleman, who looked to be in charge, was wearing a fine suit and a black homburg hat.

"They must be here about the trapped riggers," mused Joe.

"Let's eat," replied Ed'ard, pushing past his brother.

Walking over to the large bin full of fried chicken, he picked up a pair of tongs and began to sort through what little was left. "I knew it," he exclaimed, "not a short leg to be had!"

Joe poked him in the back with his finger and said, "C'mon get somethin' and let's eat."

"HELP! SOMEBODY, HELP ME!" CD screamed at the top of his lungs. No one answered. He reached a hand down to feel his leg and it was soaking wet. "*I pissed myself!*" he thought. When the car collapsed on him, he'd blacked out and now he could not remember anything. He worried about what the others would think when they found out he'd wet his britches, but smelling his fingers he realized it was blood.

A deep dread overtook him. It was blood all right and there was a lot of it. "I'm dying," he whispered to himself. He was surprised at the realization. He'd always known it would happen someday, but he figured he'd be an old man lying in his bed, surrounded by friends and family. It had never crossed his mind that this short money job would cost him his life.

He thought about the first time he'd kissed Leola at the church picnic. He remembered their first night of matrimony and the way her skin felt next to his. Memories of getting to know his son and teaching him about what it means to be a man—*a Malone man*—flooded back to his mind.

The thoughts came to him, one by one and then all at once. It was as if he was seeing them displayed as photographs pinned to a wall. It was too much and he began to weep. Somewhere in the weeping and lament, a thief broke in and stole his hope. An ugly nagging "something" crept into his mind and all thought turned to shame and accusation.

The trapped and desperate man began to regret every mistake and unkind word. All of his failures became larger and more consequential in his imagination. He was almost convinced that it would be best if he *did* die and that Leola and Pink would be better off without him.

He pulled to free himself, but the pain was too great and his strength seemed half of what it should have been.

He felt cold and suddenly all went black.

Outside of the collapsed coal car, work continued to shore it up.

"Get those timbers under there and stabilize that car," yelled the railroad foreman pointing at the gondola, "I don't want it to move even one inch!"

The crane operators and engineers finally got the boiler on the second crane up to working temperature and repositioned it beside the collapsed coal car.

They began to unreel the large steel cable, and several of the men on the rigging crew hurried to shackle it to the railroad car.

By now, it was nearly ten o'clock. The railroad foreman could see that the rigging crew was spent, "Get me twenty, fresh, able-bodied men from camp. We are going to get that man out. Dead or alive, we're not going to quit until he's out."

Doc heard the foreman ask for more men. While he couldn't argue that rested men were needed, it worried him that they were being replaced. He walked over to the railroad man and said, "Sir, we will gladly move out of the way for fresh men to take over, but we cannot leave here while one of our own is trapped under that railroad car."

CD's crew had been hard at work since seven that morning, with only a couple of breaks. The men were exhausted and hungry.

The foreman agreed, "You and your men can stay here and help as much as you are able."

In just minutes, twenty-two men arrived at the site of the collapsed car. Carrying shovels and picks, the men walked with a quickened pace and with purpose. Joe and Ed'ard walked near the front of the group. No one knew the name of the man who was trapped. When the fresh crew arrived at the site Ed'ard and Joe looked for CD among the others in the rigging crew. Not finding him, they began to ask around. Two of the crane operators were standing in a group of men who were waiting to speak to the foreman.

"I reckon those boys ought to know where CD's at," shouted Joe over the commotion. Joe walked over and tapped one of the men on the shoulder.

"Excuse me, mister," he said, "we're lookin' for our brother."

"Don't know him, son," replied the man. "We've got an emergency situation here, so clear out or help those men over there," he continued, pointing to a crew shuffling timbers over to the car.

The man turned back around, so Joe tapped him on the shoulder again. Annoyed, the man spun around and barked, "Boy, get to work or go home."

Ed'ard saw a look on Joe's face that he recognized. It was a look he'd personally put there more than once and had felt the consequences too.

Intervening Ed'ard spoke up, "Mister, our brother is on this crew. We're just trying to find him."

Joe and Ed'ard's brother was the only white man on the crew, so immediately the crane operator turned to give the brothers his full attention. "Is your brother the one they call Hillbilly?" he asked.

"Yes," hollered Joe.

The man's expression changed from agitation to concern. "Come with me."

He led Joe and Ed'ard over to another man in a suit.

"This is Mr. Batone," said the man. He looked at him and said, "These men are looking for CD Malone."

"Thank you," replied Mr. Batone, "Would you give us a minute please?"

The crane operator left, walking back to the area where the foreman was still giving orders and directing the effort to rescue CD.

"My name is Joseph Batone," said the man shaking hands with Joe and Ed'ard.

Ed'ard couldn't wait for formalities, "CD's our brother!"

"Gentlemen, I'm afraid your brother is the man trapped under the coal car," he said.

"Jesus, no!" exclaimed Joe.

"What can we do to help?" asked Ed'ard.

"It would be best if you two went back to camp and tried to get some rest." It was routine advice for situations like this, but as soon as the words left his mouth, he knew they were for naught. He looked at the Malone brothers and could tell they weren't going anywhere until they knew their brother was okay.

He relented, "Go see the foreman and tell him I said to put you to work."

"Thanks mister," said Joe, as he and Ed'ard sprinted back toward the rail car.

As Joe and Ed'ard waited with the other men to receive further instructions, they watched the men from CD's crew digging and hauling dirt and rocks from under the coal car.

One of the crane operators, after speaking with two other men, walked over to the foreman and said, "We've been talking and we think we might be able to lift the car, if we can get both winches on it."

Dr. Oden, who had overheard the entire conversation, quickly interjected, "No! Without knowing the exact position of CD, in relation to that cable, you risk tearing him in two!"

"This might be our only chance," warned the crane operator, "there's more rain coming tonight."

The railroad foreman looked at the operator and then at Dr. Oden. He paused and rubbed the back of his neck. The strain of the day's events was taking its toll on him too. He worried that his own fatigue might cloud his judgement.

"Doc's right," the railroad foreman finally replied. He nodded at Dr. Oden and told the crane operators to stand by, until the men were able to reach the trapped worker and verify that the cable was safe to retrieve.

Meanwhile, the recovery crew continued to dig under the car searching for CD, calling out for him and desperately hoping to hear a response.

As more help came to relieve the exhausted men, who hadn't taken a break since the car collapsed, the railroad foreman briefed them on the situation and made it clear that the operation would continue until CD was saved or his body recovered.

Joe looked at Ed'ard. There was intense emotion on his face. They exchanged no words... Ed'ard knew exactly what Joe's look meant. CD *had* to be alive. Nothing like this had ever happened in the Malone family before, and if CD died, it would change them forever.

"Now, I know some of you might not like the idea of working with colored men," said the foreman, "But tonight I need you to put aside any prejudices you might have. You will focus on one thing and one thing only—getting that man out of there."

All of the fresh men from the camp nodded their heads in silence and the railroad foreman continued. "If he is still alive, he may be injured and there's no way to tell how long he'll last. He's been under there since before five o'clock."

Side by side, white and black workers hauled dirt and rocks from under the rail car. They used jacks to raise it as much as possible, careful not to cause it to shift again. The number two crane's winch line was rigged onto the car, to keep it from slipping further down the muddy hillside.

Someone had started a couple of campfires and the men from the mess tent had come to set up a coffee station. The chill of the damp night air made coffee a real blessing as the men worked.

By one in the morning, most of the men on CD's crew were too exhausted to continue and had gathered by one of the fires. They were singing spiritual songs and old hymns.

Leaning, leaning, safe and secure from all alarms.
Leaning, leaning, leaning on the everlasting arms...

Chapter 17

Pearly Gates

Back in Paige County, Pink and 'Lij were doing their best to hitch Mars to the turning plow. Of the two mules on their farm, she was the most agreeable. The pair of cousins had managed to get the harness and the bridle on the mule, but convincing Mars to back up to the plow—was another matter.

Unwilling and stronger than the boys, Mars was not moving an inch. Pink walked in front of the mule and popped her between the eyes.

"Gosh almighty!" exclaimed Pink, clutching his hand in pain.

"You're gonna bust your hand," warned 'Lij.

"Maybe she'll back up if we sing to her," said Pink, "I've seen Daddy do that, a time or two."

"Uncle CD sings all the time. Ain't no mule gonna back for you, just on account of you singin' to it," replied an exasperated 'Lij.

"C'mon, 'Lij, help me," replied Pink, "She likes church songs."

The two cousins began to sing, although Elijah was still not convinced it would work.

"Oh, how sweet to walk in this pilgrim way,

Leanin' on the everlasting arms;

Oh, how bright the path grows from day to day,

Leanin' on the everlasting arms."

Lo and behold, in the time it took the boys to sing one refrain, Mars backed right up to the plow and let out a good long bray. Leola had been watching the boys from the kitchen window and walked out to take them some water. She adored Pink and was proud of him. There was really no rush to turn the soil over for the spring plant, because CD was due home in a few days. However, Leola knew that Pink was intent on proving himself. She knew that it was important for a boy, who's trying to become a man, to demonstrate that he is capable, to both his father and himself.

"Boys, that was beautiful singin'," she said as she approached Pink and 'Lij.

"Thank you Aunt Leola," replied Elijah, "But truth be told, it was pretty awful, and Mars probably only got on this plow, to make us hush up."

Leola and Pink had a good laugh, as the three of them shared the refreshing water. The day was perfect. It was sunny and cool. Pink and 'Lij had been diligent in helping one another while their fathers were away, and today they were turning over soil to expose it to the sun.

"I expect your pa is going to be quite pleased with you Pink.

Why, when he gets home and sees all the hard work you two have been doing around here, he will probably burst wide open with pride," said Leola.

Pink grinned so big it would have made a possum jealous, "Do you really think so mama?"

"Why yes. He might even put his feet up for a few days, when he arrives home," she teased.

"When are they supposed to get back from Charlottesville?" asked Elijah.

"I don't know exactly," she answered, "but it could be any day now."

When they'd finished their water, Pink and 'Lij went back to work with the mule and plow, and Leola started back to the house. On her way to the house, she found a baby redbird that had fallen out of its nest and died. *"What a shame,"* she thought. She fetched a shovel and buried it there.

As she covered the deceased bird with soil, she felt a deep sorrow. The sorrow turned to a feeling of loss and then dread. She hated that fear, that dread, that awful sadness that seemed so easily to overtake her.

She tried to chase it away with singing. *"What have I to fear, what have I to dread, leaning on the everlasting arms..."* But as soon as she stepped into the kitchen, her eyes fixed on the table. She recalled the kiss CD had given her the day he left for Charlottesville.

"Lord, watch over my Charles and bring him home to us," she prayed.

Back under the railroad car, CD could hear Saint Peter calling his name. He could hear a choir singing faintly in the distance. Saint Peter was wiping the tears from CD's face, although a few times it felt more like a slap.

"Charles Daniel Malone! Wake Up!"

"Hillbilly! C'mon, Hillbilly. You have to wake up," he said. Another slap and CD began to regain consciousness.

CD mumbled, "You're black."

Confused by CD's assessment of his skin color, he answered, "All my life."

As CD became somewhat lucid, he realized it was his friend, Jerome, who'd been slapping him.

"You hit me," murmured CD.

Jerome laughed, "Well it worked didn't it."

CD managed a frail grin but lacked the strength to return the laughter. He had been pinned under the railcar for almost ten hours. He was weak from blood loss, dehydrated, and in terrible pain.

"I'm in a bad way," CD said softly, "My leg is broke."

"C'mon," replied Jerome pulling on his shoulders, "I'm gettin' you outta here."

"My leg is pinned," CD managed, "and I'm so thirsty."

Jerome felt around in the darkness and found the large steel cable. It was under CD's back. He explained to him that he had to pull it out from under him and why.

"We need this cable to lift this coal car off you," he explained. Jerome dug with his hands and the short-handled shovel he'd brought with him until he was finally able to free the cable.

"You stay right here," said Jerome. CD tried to laugh but only managed to smile. "I'll be right back. I'm going to get help... I'll get you some water too," he said.

Jerome scrambled out from under the car, dragging the end of the cable. When he emerged, he held up the cable and yelled, "I found him. He's alive!"

Every man in earshot shouted in jubilation. The railroad foreman and Mr. Batone immediately called Jerome over to a table that had been set up in front of a truck with its headlights on.

Ed'ard and Joe followed Jerome. They were eager to hear news about their brother. Mr. Batone introduced Jerome to the brothers. Jerome began to tell them that CD was pinned and that his leg was broken.

"He said he's thirsty. I need to take him some water," he said. There was an urgency in Jerome's voice, so the railroad foreman sent him back.

As Jerome hurried away, the railroad man yelled to him, "You tell him we're gonna get him out of there."

Jerome nodded his head and took off running to get water and take it to CD. When he reached the water barrel, Dr. Oden was there and had already filled a flask.

Doc smiled at Jerome and slapped him on the back, "I knew you would find him. I never had a doubt."

He looked at Doc with intense worry on his face. "He's bad off...*real* bad off."

Doc reached out and put a hand on his shoulder to assure him, "He's gonna make it. The Lord hasn't brought him this far, only to quit on him now. Now go on and tell Hillbilly he is going to be just fine."

Jerome ran to the entrance of the small tunnel the men had dug and disappeared under the gondola. Dr. Oden was overwhelmed. He was dog-tired and barely able to stand. As an academic, he was not as fit as the other men were. He was used to teaching in a classroom, not performing hard manual labor. Of all the men on the rigging crew, he was the most visibly exhausted.

He turned around and surveyed the scene. There were already men scaling the collapsed railcar, working to secure the second winch cable. Some men were positioning timbers to shore up the car in preparation for when the cranes lifted it. Some were standing by waiting for instructions, while some of the men on the rigging crew had returned to their singing.

Dr. Oden walked over to the group of riggers who were singing and said, "Men, your music is angelic, but I think our breath would be best spent in prayer at the moment."

The men moved from around the campfire and formed a small circle and Doc began to pray. As the men from CD's rigging crew prayed, one by one many other men walked over, removed their hats, and stood with them in prayer.

When Jerome reached CD again, he was still awake. Jerome took the cork out of the flask and said, "Here, take some water."

CD drank the water and closed his eyes. No taste of water had ever been as sweet. Jerome barely fit under the space where CD was trapped. He lay there beside CD and gave an audible sigh. He was used up and his body ached all over from hours of frantically laboring to save his comrade.

"If you don't mind sharing a room with me, I think I'll try to get a nap," said Jerome jokingly.

"You sleep all you want," rasped CD, "I ain't goin' nowhere."

Jerome laughed and then he felt a hand grasp his arm.

"You gotta do somethin' for me Jerome," whispered CD, "You gotta tell my Leola that I love her so," CD's voice wavered a bit. "You tell her—there ain't no one else for me."

Jerome didn't know what to say. He'd never seen a man die before. "Okay," he replied, "I'll tell her."

When Jerome did not return from under the collapsed coal car, the railroad foreman sent another man in to see what was wrong. When he finally managed to crawl in to where Jerome and CD were, he said, "Hey, you need to get outta here so they can lift this car!"

Jerome never moved. He lay there on his back, next to CD, and replied, "Well, you tell 'em to go on and move it then. I ain't goin' anyplace."

"They say the car could slip and fall again, you'll be killed," argued the man.

"Then I'll give Hillbilly a personal escort to heaven," he replied, "But I ain't leavin' him!"

Emerging from under the railcar, the man relayed what Jerome had told him and Mr. Batone gave the order to raise the car.

"If that car slips and falls again, that'll be two deaths the railroad will be accountable for," protested the foreman.

Mr. Batone set his jaw and said sternly, "*I* wouldn't leave that man under there alone... would you?"

"No," agreed the foreman. He turned from Mr. Batone and whirling his finger above his head in a circle gave the order, "Raise her up!"

Three dozen men stood at the ready with timbers so they could shore up the car as soon as it cleared the ground.

The two crane operators engaged their winches and began to reel in the steel cables. Slowly the car inched up off the ground and then a foot more. As the cranes reeled in their winch lines, the car came further off the ground. As it cleared more ground, the workers stacked timbers under it to ensure it could not collapse again.

The cables tightened, the tension made them chirp and sing. The engines on the cranes belched thick black smoke and hissed steam. By this time, all hands were on deck. An ambulance truck was on station and a surgeon was waiting at the hospital in town.

All at once, the car jerked upward and released its prisoner. Jerome rolled over and prepared to drag CD out from under the gondola, the second he was free.

Yelling over the noise of the cranes, he shouted at CD, "Look here. When this car gets off your leg, I'm gonna drag you out from under here. It's gonna hurt mighty bad!"

CD nodded and closed his eyes. Suddenly, the headlights from one of the trucks at the work site shined in Jerome's face. All the men cheered as Jerome began to drag the hillbilly from under the coal car. In a mere twelve feet, Jerome and CD were clear of the car. As roughly as he'd handled him, CD didn't make a sound. Jerome looked down to ask him if he was okay and CD did not respond. He was unconscious again.

Ambulance workers hurriedly loaded CD into the truck and raced to the hospital.

When Jerome saw the ambulance leave, he smiled and then collapsed sitting down on the ground. He sat there with his knees bent and his hands and head resting on them. Silently he was praying, crying, singing, shouting, dancing, and exhausted all at the same time. He heard someone shout his name, and turned his head to see Dr. Oden holding out a hand to help him up.

"You did it!" he exclaimed, "You did it. God bless you, son, you did it."

Chapter 18

The News

"What a lovely dress, Mary Ethel," said Leola.

"Why thank you," she replied, "I finished it yesterday afternoon, and I just couldn't wait to wear it to church."

"You are such a skilled seamstress. I should come by and take more lessons," Leola added.

Warner and a dozen or so men were standing under a beech tree, a fair distance from the church doors. They were laughing and carryin' on, quite loudly. Some were enjoying their last cigarette before the service began. One of the deacons was telling a joke—waving his arms and dancing in a circle.

At the sound of laughter bursting forth from the group of men, Leola and Mary Ethel turned to see what all the commotion was about.

"Heaven knows what goes on in the mind of a man," said

Mary Ethel. "After almost 40 years, I still marvel at how boyish mine can be."

"I see that in Charles sometimes too," replied Leola.

Mary Ethel smiled, "I suppose it's their way of trying to hold on to their youth."

"I found a dead bird yesterday morning," Leola blurted out.

The abrupt manner in which she had changed the subject, caught Mary Ethel off guard. Leola's entire demeanor had changed. She went from cheery and light, to gloomy and burdened. To Leola's friends and family, she always seemed unshakeable. Growing up, she'd learned to pick up the expectations of others and become whatever was most acceptable. She instinctively knew how to adapt to just about any environment she found herself in.

Today, however, she slipped and let Mary Ethel through the gateway into her inner turmoil.

Sensing an opportunity for a mother-daughter talk, Mary Ethel hooked her arm inside of her daughter-in-law's, and said, "Let's me and you go for a walk."

"What about church," Leola protested.

Mary Ethel chuckled, "Oh, I expect they'll carry on without us just fine." She waved at Warner, who was still talking and laughing with the other men, "We're goin' for a walk together, we'll meet you back here after a while."

Warner waved back and she and Leola began their stroll.

As soon as they were out of earshot of the church, Leola began to tell Mary Ethel all about how well Pink was doing with his daddy gone. She talked about the way he'd been going to bed early and getting up before sunrise to start his chores.

"You know that boy even got Elijah to help him hitch up the plow so he could have some of the ground turned over before Charles gets home," said Leola.

"Pink is a fine boy, just like his daddy, and he'll be a fine man someday," said Mary Ethel. "But it isn't Pink that has you so worried, is it?"

Leola didn't answer but instead continued talking about Pink. Mary Ethel let her carry on for a while about nothing, and everything, except what was really on her mind.

As they walked, she took her time making sure Leola had every opportunity to open up. She stopped often to examine wild flowers and dogwood blossoms hoping Leola would unload her burden.

But fear often holds a grip so firm that even on the threshold of liberation, its prisoner may wince at the thought of being set free. Mary Ethel, being older and much wiser, knew the value of leading Leola out of her captivity, rather than dragging her against her will. Many who are coerced into abandoning anxiety, simply return to it later. It can become a familiar companion of sorts. However, fear is never a *good* companion... never kind... never considerate, always cruel and abusive.

Like a mother with her beloved child, Mary Ethel kept Leola company and offered her the freedom to just *be*. As they carried on together, they arrived at a place where the railroad tracks came near. Both Leola and Mary Ethel noticed the tracks, at almost the same time. Leola did not mention the tracks. Which was precisely why Mary Ethel *did* mention them. She suspected CD being gone was what had her so worried.

"Strange thing about train tracks... they come and go, but they never move. They bring, they carry away, yet they have no arms or legs. They are wonderful, and at the same time terrible, it just depends on what or who, is coming or going," Mary Ethel said.

"Mary Ethel, do you think I'm pretty?" asked Leola. There was a sadness in her tone that told Mary Ethel that she had already answered that question for herself, long ago.

"Goodness me child! Of course, you are. What on earth would make you doubt a thing like that?" she asked in reply.

Leola looked at the ground and replied, "I don't know... I guess I'm just being silly. Let's go back, I suppose church is nearly over by now." She was already regretting her question but it was too late.

"Leola, I don't think you're silly. I think you're one of the loveliest girls in this county," said Mary Ethel.

Leola looked up at her with a worried hurt on her face. "That's just it. Maybe I am pretty compared to others around here, but do you think if Charles had better to choose from that he would have still picked me?" she asked.

"Leola, if CD hadn't grabbed you up when he did, a dozen other boys would have. But that's beside the point. Warner and I were there; the first time he saw you at the church. That boy was never the same and spent every waking moment, from that day until he married you, trying to figure out a way to be 'round you. He'd have married you that very day, if we'd have let him," she answered.

Leola turned away. She was beginning to cry, not because her mother-in-law's words were so sweet, but because she didn't believe them and they irritated her tormenting companion—fear. The place in us where fear goes to hide and destroy hope is beyond the reach of kind words. It lies safely hidden behind years of practiced worry and self-doubt, and its final destruction must be a work from within.

"He's a good man," said Leola softly. What she really meant was, "too good for me".

Realizing that perhaps Leola had gone as far as she dared, Mary Ethel said, "Why don't we start back to the church."

When they reached the church, Leola and Mary Ethel could hear the final hymn. The members formed a motley choir, but the noise was beautiful and comforting.

"I have blessed peace with my Lord so near,

Leaning on the everlasting arms."

They stepped into the church through the opened doors and stood with the others as the service concluded.

After the service was over, a deacon came and got Mary Ethel and Leola. He led them back to the pastor's office where the sheriff was waiting with his hat in his hands. He looked worried but gave a smile and greeted the ladies.

"Mrs. Mary Ethel... Mrs. Leola," he said nodding his head.

"What is this about?" asked Mary Ethel.

"CD's been in an accident," said Gordy.

Leola's face became pale and she gasped putting her hands over her mouth.

Sheriff Edwards held up a hand and continued, "But I was told he's going to be just fine. He's in the hospital in Charlottesville. He has a broken leg and a few other scrapes and bruises, but the doctor says he will make a full recovery."

Leola turned to Mary Ethel and said, "I need to go to him. I-I-I don't know what to do. How will I get there? What about Pink, and the farm? What about the animals?"

The news was hard to take, and she was panicking. Mary Ethel did her best to reassure Leola that everything would be fine.

Gordy explained that the railroad company had arranged transportation for her, at no expense.

"The fella on the telephone said that you are to be at the railway station in Luray tomorrow morning at seven. They made arrangements with the Norfolk and Western to get you to Waynesboro and then on to Charlottesville. There'll be a man there waiting to take you to the hospital to see your husband," explained Sheriff Edwards.

Leola turned to Mary Ethel and asked, "Will you go with me?"

"Of course, I will. We'll take a nice train ride together, see the countryside, and then CD," she answered. "Do try not to fret dear, I'm sure that in short order, CD is gonna be right as rain."

As Leola and Mary Ethel stepped from the pastor's office into the sanctuary, they were amazed to see one of the deacons leading everyone in a special time of prayer for CD and their family. Nearly everyone had stayed behind to pray for him.

The deacon called on Warner to pray, and suddenly Warner found himself in a public pickle. He didn't mind praying, in fact, he prayed every morning and every night but never in front of people and especially not out loud.

Warner was ready to politely refuse, when he caught Mary Ethel's eye. She gave him a look that said both, "I'm so proud of you, and you'd better do it."

Stepping up behind the pulpit, Warner nervously began, "Lord, you're mighty good to us and my boy CD is a mighty good man. He's in a hospital in Charlottesville, Virginia with a broken leg. He's in a mighty bad way. Lord, we ask you to be with Leola and Pink and help them be strong. It's a mighty long way down there, please make a way for us to get him home. Amen."

When Warner left the pulpit, he walked over to where Mary Ethel and Leola were standing at the back of the church.

"How'd I do," he whispered.

"It was a 'mighty' fine prayer," Mary Ethel teased.

When the prayer service concluded, Sheriff Edwards offered to drive Leola and Pink home, she declined, however, thinking that it might be better if she and Pink had some time alone to talk about what had happened.

On the walk home, she told Pink what little she knew, and that in the morning his Grandma Mary Ethel would accompany her down to Charlottesville to see his daddy.

"Which of his leg bones got broke?" asked Pink.

"Broken, dear heart, 'Which of his leg bones got *broken*,'" she corrected, before answering Pink's question. "I don't know, but if he's in the hospital, it must be a clean break and not just a crack."

Pink stopped in the road, ran his hands up and down his leg, and tried to feel the bone he imagined his pa had broken.

"If it's one of these on the bottom that'll be better, 'cause we got two down there," he proffered.

"I don't know, Son," she replied.

The pair walked the rest of the way home with little more than small talk. Pink did not seem phased at all by the news about his daddy. It may have been his boyish immaturity or something else. In any case, his calm demeanor was a comfort to his mother.

When they got home, Pink spent the rest of the afternoon tending to the chickens and other livestock before walking over to 'Lij's place to throw baseballs.

"Your daddy gonna be alright?" asked 'Lij.

"Sheriff Edwards said he heard he's gonna be fine, once his leg bone knits," replied Pink.

"What will y'all do about plantin'?"

Pink thought about it hard for a minute, and replied, "I don't know. I wonder if I could do it."

"Ain't no way," replied Elijah. "Me and you barely got two

acres turned over last week. It'll take a heap more muscle than me and you got."

Leola and Elijah's mother decided that Pink would sleep over at Lij's, while Leola was away. Leola needed the assurance that Pink would be taken care of, but still close enough to keep up his chores at home.

In the morning, Warner and Mary Ethel fetched Leola to the train station in Luray. It was only a half hour or so by wagon and the morning's air was dry and warm.

Arriving at the station, Warner accompanied the ladies to the ticket counter and they explained that there was an arrangement for her to travel down to Waynesboro on the seven AM train.

The ticket master tipped his cap, and said, "I have a telegram here that says I'm to put a Mrs. Leola Malone on the train, in first class, right up next to the dining car." Poking his chest out with pride, he continued, "All meals and beverages are compliments of the Norfolk and Western ma'am."

"Thank you so kindly," replied Leola, "But my mother-in-law is traveling with me to keep me company."

The man leaned down to whisper, trying not to offend Mary Ethel, "Nobody said anything to me about a mother-in-law."

Warner thought to himself, that the man must have learned to whisper in a sawmill, because he heard every word, from twenty feet away. "How much is the ticket?" Warner asked.

The ticket master looked surprised that Warner had heard him, "Well, to Waynesboro it's sixty-five cents."

Warner reached for his coin purse and as he did the man

stopped him, "Sir, I reckon the railroad can spare one more seat." He produced a second ticket and handed it to Mary Ethel.

"God bless you, mister," said Warner.

The man smiled and then addressed Leola, "Ma'am, is your husband the fella that was buried alive in that accident, where they're cleaning up after the train derailment in Charlottesville?"

"Buried alive?" she gasped.

"I do hope he will be alright," he added.

"Thank you. We'd better get out to the platform," said Mary Ethel leading Leola away by the arm.

"Don't pay him any mind," said Mary Ethel, "rumors are like weeds... they spring up and choke the life out of everything. CD's gonna be fine."

Leola managed a strained smile, and replied, "I'm sure you're right."

Chapter 19

Acres of Gratitude

"Well, it won't hurt to ask," Doc said, "all the man can do is refuse. He can't take away your birthday or shave your head and make you join the Marines."

Jerome thought it over. He knew Dr. Oden was right, but he still thought it would be best if Doc did the asking.

"Would you ask him for me?" he replied.

Doc smiled and gave him a playful punch on the shoulder, "It would be my pleasure."

During lunch, Dr. Oden spotted the railroad foreman sitting under a tree. He was eating cold, fried chicken from a picnic basket and drinking hot coffee from a large vacuum flask.

As the railroad foreman watched Dr. Oden approach, he noticed how formally he carried himself. He studied his gate and the swing of his arms. He was impressed, yes, even intimidated, by Doc's good manners, large vocabulary, and steady confidence.

"Mr. Rogerson, I wonder if we might have a word with you?" Doc asked.

"Sure thing," said the foreman, "What's on your mind, and call me Clem."

Doc began to speak, but Clem cut him off, "I meant to tell you 'thank you' for what you did the other night. If you hadn't insisted that we wait to reel the winch cable back, that man would have been torn in two."

"It wasn't anything any man wouldn't have done," Doc replied.

Mr. Rogerson smiled, and said, "Yet... yet, you're the only man who spoke up."

Doc nodded his head and accepted his gratitude.

"Now what's on your mind?" asked Clem.

Doc took his hat off, and with his handkerchief, wiped the sweat from his brow.

"Well, sir," he began, "Jerome would very much like to visit CD at the hospital. And yes, I do understand the sensitive nature of the request."

Clem visibly grimaced at the thought of trying to get Jerome into the hospital to visit a white patient. "Doc, I don't know," he hesitated. "Tell you what," he continued, "this evening, after supper, I'll ride you and Jerome over there, but you have to do all the talking."

"Alright then," said Doc smiling, "Consider me your personal orator."

After the evening meal, Doc and Jerome met Mr. Rogerson where he'd instructed. They climbed onto the back of the truck and he drove them into town.

Arriving at the hospital, Clem parked the truck and got out. Doc and Jerome jumped down and walked up to the sidewalk. After joining them, Clem offered, "Now I can get you fellas in the door, but you're on your own after that."

Doc nodded, and the trio entered the building. Mr. Rogerson waited just inside the doorway while Doc and Jerome approached the nurse at the front desk.

The nurse looked a little surprised to see the men, but she managed to maintain a polite demeanor.

"May I help you?" she asked.

Taking off his hat, Doc replied, "Yes ma'am, I hope so. My name is Dr. Kevin Oden, and this is my companion, Mr. Jerome Braswell."

The nurse nodded and let Doc continue.

"You have a patient here by the name of Charles Daniel Malone..."

Jerome interjected, "We just call him CD."

Doc smiled, "Yes...CD. My friend and I would very much like to visit him, for just a few minutes."

"Gentlemen," the nurse replied, "I'm afraid that is completely out of the question."

Doc held his hat in both hands in front of his chest. "Ma'am, CD is a member of our crew at the train derailment worksite. We're only asking for five minutes to pass along the well wishes of his workmates."

"I'm sorry," she replied, "but there's nothing I can do."

Doc looked at the nurse and then at Jerome. The look on Jerome's face was almost as determined as when he'd begun digging to find CD under the collapsed gondola.

"Pardon me, Miss—but Jerome here is the one who tunneled under that rail car and saved that man's life," pleaded Doc.

The nurse looked stunned and gasped, "Oh, my Lord!" She looked down the hallway, and seeing no one, whispered, "Come with me."

She led them to a set of stairs, near the back of the building, and asked, "Do you have a watch?"

Dr. Oden smiled, "But of course."

"Okay," she continued, "now wait inside the stairwell for two minutes, then go to the second floor and meet me outside of room 217."

Dr. Oden and Jerome made their way up the stairs as quickly, and as quietly, as possible. Peering from the door, Jerome scanned up the hallway. There were a few nurses making rounds, but for the most part, the hallway was empty and quiet.

Finding the door to room 217 closed, the pair waited outside, when all of a sudden, the nurse from the reception desk, flung it open and whispered, "In here, hurry."

Doc and Jerome stepped inside the room; there lay CD with a bandage around his head and a tube in his arm. The doctors had set the bone in his leg and splinted it. It hung in the air from a trapeze. He was awake, but his eyes looked heavy and his face seemed weary.

The nurse walked over to him and said, "Mr. Malone, you have visitors." Before the nurse left the room, she stopped at the door and held up five fingers. Dr. Oden nodded toward the nurse and said, "Five minutes...yes ma'am."

Doc motioned for Jerome to speak, "Make it quick," he said.

When CD saw him, a tear streamed down his face. Jerome nodded his head, acknowledging what both men felt. The weight of the past days' events had taken their toll.

"All the fellas send their regards," said Jerome.

CD smiled and replied, "Tell 'em thank you, and tell 'em— they *might* have to finish up without me."

Doc smiled and Jerome laughed.

CD reached for the side table and picked up his pocket watch. He gripped it in his fist and then opened the case. He studied the inscription and closed it. Holding out the watch, he said, "Here."

"What is that?" asked Jerome.

"It's my timepiece. I want you to have it— a small 'thank you' for savin' my life," he replied. He paused and then continued, "I thought I was dead and that you were Saint Peter."

Grinning, Jerome replied, "Well, what you thought was the Pearly Gates, turned out to be my pearly whites."

Doc and CD both laughed aloud.

As Jerome examined the watch, CD apologized for it being "gold filled" and not *all* gold.

Jerome laughed, "Where'd a hillbilly get a watch this fancy?"

"Leola—I mean...my wife, gave it to me on our wedding day," he replied.

Jerome flipped the case open and inside the lid was an inscription: "*To my darling Charles. Love, Leola.*"

Handing the pocket watch back to CD, Jerome said, "Well, if you like sleepin' indoors, I expect you better keep this. I appreciate it, but I don't need anything. The Lord has been plenty good to me and my family."

Doc cleared his throat, to let Jerome know it was time for them to leave, and waved at CD. Returning a smile, CD said, "Doc, I'm sure glad to have met you."

"I'm glad to have met you too, Hillbilly," he replied grinning.

Doc cracked open the door and checked to ensure that it was clear, before motioning for Jerome to follow.

As Jerome put his hand on the door to leave, CD called out, "Land...I have land!"

Jerome turned around and asked, "What?"

CD pushed himself up, as high as he could with his elbows, and said, "I have land. It's good land, bottom country, rich, and fertile as any you've seen. I can give you land to farm."

Jerome let go of the door and walked back over to CD. "Land?" he asked, "Are you on the level?"

Outside in the hallway, Doc was getting anxious. He expected that Jerome would be right behind him. A few more nurses had come up the stairs to check on patients. One of the orderlies noticed Doc and walked over to inquire as to why he was there.

"Mister, can I help you?" asked the man. There was an incredulous tone in his voice.

"I'm Dr. Kevin Oden," he replied, "My associate and I are here representing the railroad company on behalf of Mr. Charles Daniel Malone."

The orderly looked confused, "Well, the railroad people have done been here already, and they ain't said nothin' about nobody else comin'. Especially nobody colored."

Doc put a hand on his hip and with the other rubbed his chin, "I see, that is actually not surprising. The railroad has so many men working on this derailment that sometimes the right hand, doesn't know what the left hand is doing."

"Hmmm, I suppose so," said the orderly.

Doc assured the man that all was well and that he and his associate would be leaving shortly. As the orderly opened the door and disappeared down the stairs, Doc gave CD's door a kick with his heel.

Inside the room, Jerome knew he had to get out of there before their presence caused them real trouble, but he couldn't believe the offer CD was making him.

"Well, you did save my life. I figure some acreage to farm would say 'thank you' better than a pocket watch," CD continued.

Jerome could hardly believe what he'd heard, "You sure that ain't the laudanum talkin'?"

CD grinned as big as the Shenandoah Valley and replied, "No sir, I mean it. If you want it...I will see to it that you have land to farm and make a livin' out of."

Jerome shook his hand, "Alright then, it's decided. I accept. How long is your offer good for?"

"As long as you live!" CD replied. "It'd be nice to have another good man for a neighbor."

Jerome held the handshake and looked CD in the eyes, "You *are* a good man Charles Daniel Malone."

"Takes one to know one, ain't that what they say?" he replied.

When Jerome emerged from the room, Dr. Oden was standing by the door to the stairs. He looked at Jerome and waved at him to hurry. The pair clomped their way down the stairs, now unconcerned about all the noise. Unable to contain his excitement, Jerome shouted, "He's gonna give me some land!"

Doc stopped at the bottom of the stairs. "Land?" he asked.

Beaming, Jerome replied, "Yep, CD said he's got land and he'll give me some to farm and live on."

Doc smiled. He was extraordinarily happy for Jerome, and for CD, "He's different, that one."

Peering from the stairwell door into the foyer, Jerome whispered back, "Sure is. The world could use more like him."

Chapter 20

Wildflowers

When the train arrived in Waynesboro, Mary Ethel and Leola went inside the station and checked in with the man at the ticket counter. The C&O Railroad had made all of the necessary arrangements and the ticket agent even had a second ticket available, in the event that Leola had a travelling companion.

After greeting the two ladies, the ticket agent explained: "I was instructed to provide a ticket for a Mrs. Leola Malone, so that she could visit her husband in the hospital, and to have ready an additional ticket for a companion."

As he handed Leola the tickets, he looked at Mary Ethel and remarked, "I can only assume this lovely young lady is your traveling partner?"

Mary Ethel smiled at the man and said, "God bless you, sir."

She looked down at the ticket, it had the word "Pullman" stamped on it under Accommodations.

"Excuse me, sir" Mary Ethel said, "What is Pullman?"

The ticket agent smiled. Her question told him that she had never ridden a train in luxury class before. He leaned forward on the counter, placing both elbows on the table and said, "Well, ma'am, Pullman is the company that builds and operates our luxury dining and sleeper cars. They pay us to couple them to our trains. It is the most luxurious way you can travel by rail. Oh, and if you need anything just ask the porter...he'll fetch it for you. No charge."

The generosity of the railroad overwhelmed Leola, but it also gave her tormenting companion an opportunity to prick her heart with fear. She wondered if the C&O Railroad Company was being so nice to her because CD was worse off than they'd said.

Mary Ethel, stunned at hearing they would be riding luxury class, thanked the man and then asked, "Sir, could you recommend a place, close by, where we could rest and maybe have a cup of coffee before our train arrives."

Pointing in the direction of a small cafe just up the street, the man answered, "Right over there is a cafe from which you can see the platform. You ladies will be able to see the train when it pulls into the station."

"Thank you, sir," replied Leola. "You have been most kind."

The walk to the cafe only took a few minutes. Sitting down at an outside table, Mary Ethel picked up a small paper menu from under the salt and pepper shakers.

Leola slid her chair over beside her to share the menu. It featured the usual fair one might expect at a train station café, but one thing caught Leola's eye.

"Oh, my Lord," she exclaimed in disgust, "Who on earth would ever eat cold ox tongue?"

"Where do you see that?" asked Mary Ethel.

Pointing at the menu, she replied, "Right there, under sandwiches."

Mary Ethel made an ugly face and shook her head, "The only people I know who'd eat something like that is Warner and Joe. Those two will try anything once."

Leola chuckled a bit but felt guilty and immediately stifled her laughter.

"It's still okay to laugh and enjoy yourself," said Mary Ethel.

"I know," she replied, "I just want to be strong for CD when I see him."

Mary Ethel slid her arm through Leola's and put her head on her shoulder in a hug. "I'm sure that all CD wants is to see you. In fact, I'd bet everything on it."

Even though Leola and Mary Ethel had eaten breakfast earlier that morning, they both spotted the blueberry pie on the dessert menu.

"Where do you suppose they found blueberries, this early in the spring?" asked Leola.

Mary Ethel smiled and said, "I don't have any idea, but if they have them, I expect we should give their pie a taste."

They both ordered coffee and blueberry pie. When the pie and coffee was served they looked at each other as if to ask,

"Should we give thanks?" Mary Ethel offered to say a blessing over their snack and the two bowed their heads.

"Dear Lord, thank you for this fine weather, fine company, and for the generosity of the railroad. Bless this pie to the nourishment of our bodies and us to thy service for Christ's sake. Amen."

Leola took a bite of the pie and immediately smiled. "It's delightful," she said.

Mary Ethel made it known to Leola that she found the pie a bit lacking. Leola assumed it may have been because Mary Ethel fancied herself an expert when it came to baking pies. For the next hour or so, she and Mary Ethel debated the finer points of baking the perfect blueberry pie. Their waitress had refilled their coffee, at least twice, at no additional charge and had offered a secret or two of her own about baking. While they sat talking, the train to Charlottesville sounded its whistle as it entered the town of Waynesboro.

"That'd be our train I expect," said Mary Ethel.

She produced a quarter from her pocketbook and left it on the table. "That should do nicely," she said.

When they boarded the train, they presented their passes to the conductor who signaled the Pullman porter to escort them to their private compartment.

The two ladies entered the compartment and were stunned at its exquisite appointments. The seats were a rich, dark, green velvet that folded out into beds. Stained mahogany wainscoting and beautiful floral printed paper adorned the walls. Every latch, handle, and knob was polished brass and lush carpeting covered the floor from wall to wall. There was even a lavatory and a sink with running water.

The trip to Charlottesville was beautiful. Along the way, the train passed fields full of wildflowers, enormous red barns, and more cattle than Leola or Mary Ethel had ever seen.

Just before the train got to Rockfish Gap, it passed a field full of bluebells and trout lilies. Hues of blue and gold blended like musical notes in a perfect song. Leola tapped Mary Ethel on the arm to get her attention.

Pointing out toward the wild flowers she said, "Those are the same kind of flowers Charles gave me when he asked for my hand."

"I remember that," said Mary Ethel. "He brought them in the house and asked me to help him fix them up." She laughed, remembering how nervous CD had been. "Why, he fussed over those flowers like he was fixin' to give them to a princess," she added.

Mary Ethel's words were a salve to Leola—like camphor on a weary back. The burdens she carried were awful and heavy. She stared at the field of wildflowers until they were out of site, all the while remembering the shaking, stuttering, eighteen-year-old on bended knee, asking for her hand in marriage. She smiled to herself, and tried to imagine her and Charles as an elderly couple, still in love, still dancing after sunset, surrounded by grandchildren.

As the train steamed on through the Blue Ridge, it rocked the ladies to sleep.

After a while, the whistle blew three times, loudly announcing the train's arrival into the Charlottesville station. The two Malone ladies awakened from their napping and began to collect their things.

Mary Ethel, sensing Leola's worry, did her best to be cheery. "Oh, I just can't wait to get over to the hospital and see CD," she chirped.

"Yes, I'm sure he will be glad to see you...us, I mean," replied Leola.

Once on the platform, Leola noticed a well-dressed man holding a white placard that simply read, "Malone."

She looked at Mary Ethel and grinned. They were being given the royal treatment and the experience was grand.

Walking over to the gentleman with the sign, Mary Ethel introduced themselves, "We are the Malones," she stated. "My name is Mary Ethel and this is my daughter-in-law, Leola."

"Good afternoon, ladies," the man said. "My name is Nathan Powell. I will be driving you from the station to the University Hospital. I will see to your bags, if you would like to wait for me inside."

"Thank you," replied Leola. She and Mary Ethel walked inside the station and found a seat on a bench. After a few minutes, Mr. Powell came into the station house followed by a pair of men who were carrying the women's luggage. Once inside, Mr. Powell instructed their bags be placed in the car waiting outside by the curb. He turned to Mary Ethel and Leola and quite formally said, "Ladies, if you will accompany me, executives from the Chesapeake and Ohio Railroad Company would like to speak with you."

"Yes, of course," replied Leola.

Mr. Powell smiled, "Excellent. Right this way please."

He led them to an office in the train station where two men in grey pin striped suits were waiting. With a quick rap on the door, Mr. Powell led the ladies into the room. He stepped to the side, gesturing with his hand open and palm facing up, and introduced them to the men.

"Gentlemen, this is Mrs. Leola Malone and her mother-in-law Mrs. Mary Ethel Malone."

The taller of the two men thanked Mr. Powell and excused him. He shook Leola's hand and said, "Mrs. Malone, my name is Joseph Batone. I work for the C&O in our Salvage and Recovery Division."

Nodding toward the other man, he continued, "And this is J. Thaddeus Forbes, my associate."

"Nice to meet you both," replied Leola. "I don't mean to be impolite, but when can I see Charles?"

Mr. Batone smiled and nodded his head. He had anticipated that CD's wife would be eager to see him, but there were particulars to go over first.

"Yes ma'am," he replied. "I fully understand. There are just a few items to cover before we part company."

Motioning to the other railroad man, he turned the conversation over to him saying, "Mr. Forbes."

"Certainly," he replied. "While you are here, we have reserved accommodations for you in our executive suite at the Colonial Inn. It is directly across the street from the hospital.

The hotel has a dining room and serves meals three times daily. If you prefer to take your meals in your room, please just phone down to the reception desk and they will make the arrangements for you. Coffee and baked goods are available throughout the day. There is also a telephone in the room for your convenience. Just pick up the receiver and someone will be on the line to assist you."

Reaching into the inside pocket of his jacket he added, "Here is my business card. If you will, kindly produce this when you require anything, and it will be charged to the railroad's account at the inn. The C&O will cover all expenses while you are our guests."

He looked at Mr. Batone and said, "Well, I think that covers the particulars." Then turning to the ladies he asked, "Do you have any questions for me?"

Mary Ethel nudged Leola and raised her eyebrows. Leola smiled. The railroad company was being so generous, it hardly seemed real. "No, sir," Leola replied.

Mr. Forbes took a seat in a wing-backed chair and crossed an ankle over his knee.

Walking over and leaning on the desk, Mr. Batone reached in his pocket, and produced a silver case. Retrieving a cigarette, he asked, "Do you mind if I smoke?"

Mary Ethel and Leola shook their heads, "No."

"Thank you," he replied, striking a match off the top of the desk. He lit the cigarette and blew the smoke away from the ladies.

"Mrs. Malone, on behalf of the Chesapeake and Ohio Railroad Company. Please allow me to extend our deepest regrets over your husband's accident. I want to assure you that all of his medical bills will be sent to the railroad and will be paid in full."

He shifted his position, flicked the ashes from the cigarette into a tray on the desk, and continued, "Mrs. Malone your husband is a fortunate man. My understanding is that he crawled under an overturned coal car, attempting to attach a steel rope so that it could be righted and restored to the train tracks, but the muddy hillside gave way and it collapsed on top of him."

Leola put a hand over her mouth as Mary Ethel clutched the other.

Mr. Batone continued to relate more details, "He was trapped under the coal car for nearly ten hours and you should know that the men on his crew, who had already worked a full day, refused to rest until he was freed."

He smiled, and putting out his cigarette, stood up from the desk. He winced at what he was about to say and chose his words carefully to avoid causing the ladies further distress.

"Mrs. Malone," he began, "I was not there when your husband became trapped, but I *was* there when he was pulled to safety. I have never witnessed anything like it. There were men digging and working feverishly to free your husband, of course, but there were also many men praying and singing hymns. But...*something else*—there was something else. There was something in the air, or maybe in the atmosphere, that I could not see, but we all could feel. Ladies, well... I'm not a church-going man, but after all this, I just might be."

Mary Ethel and Leola stood and thanked Mr. Batone for his

kind words and for the railroad's hospitality. He shook their hands and told them that Mr. Powell was waiting outside to drive them to the hospital, where they would be able to visit CD. He saw them out of the office and closed the door. Lighting another cigarette, he sat down in the chair, opened a drawer, and poured himself a glass of whiskey.

He put his feet up on the desk and as he leaned back in the chair, in his mind, he could hear the men singing on the night of CD's rescue—*he could see the whole scene again*— and he thought to himself, "*I wonder if the Man upstairs could ever love me too?*"

Chapter 21

The Most Beautiful Woman

"Is there anything else I can do for you, ladies?" asked the bellhop.

"No sir...oh wait, yes, can you please tell us when supper is served?" asked Mary Ethel.

The bellhop responded, "The restaurant is open at seven in the morning all day until nine in the evening. You may take your meals at your convenience."

"Thank you so much," replied Leola, as she turned to smile at Mary Ethel in amazement.

"You're quite welcome. If you require anything else, just phone down to the reception desk," he replied, as he left through the door.

"Well, are you ready?" asked Mary Ethel.

Leola straightened her frame and wrung her hands. Her companion was back, or more aptly, had never left. Self-doubting fear is a great and loathsome mystery. It is more than just an emotional response to perceived threats or peril. Leola's fear had been long borne in her heart from the time she was a little girl.

Her fear was as real to her as anything, and although it was horrible and abusive, it was familiar and something of a friend —*a backstabbing disloyal friend.*

One disapproving word after another from her drunken father had stolen her security and confidence. Leola's tender heart did not know how to cope or fend off such attacks, and since she loved her father, she had unconsciously made an agreement with the words he spoke over her. His inebriated hatefulness had set her tiny soul on a lifelong journey to find and recover what she had lost.

In the seconds after Mary Ethel reminded her that it was time to go see CD, Leola's heart panicked at the possibility that he might have changed his mind about her in the days since he left Paige Valley to work in Charlottesville.

Fear taunted her all at once with spontaneous imaginations of beautiful, educated nurses fawning over Charles in the hospital. In her mind, she could see young, fair-skinned nurses with golden locks and rosy cheeks, attractive figures, and perfect smiles.

In her imagination, he was all the while comparing her to them, dreaming of exchanging her for youth and beauty. So distressed by her fantasies was Leola that she did not even notice that she had begun to silently weep. The tear that tracked its way down her cheek to the corner of her mouth was salty, and forced her from her musings as she realized that Mary Ethel was staring at her.

"Dear child, where on earth are you?" asked Mary Ethel.

Snapping out of her daydream, Leola replied, "I'm right here."

Deciding it was better to let sleeping dogs lie, Mary Ethel did not pursue the matter. She took Leola by the arm and the pair made their way to the electric lift where a young man, who looked to be around twelve years old, assisted them into the car. The liftboy took them to the first-floor lobby and escorted them off the elevator. He held out his hand and Leola shook it thanking him.

Walking a good distance away, Leola said, "I've never seen anyone ask for a handshake with their hand flat like that."

Mary Ethel chuckled, "Leola, I think he was expecting a tip."

She gasped, "Oh my, I hope I didn't offend him. Should I go back and give him a penny?"

"No," Mary Ethel replied, "When we see him later, we'll just give him two."

In the lobby, Mr. Powell, from the railroad, was waiting to escort them to the hospital, but the ladies politely declined pointing out that it was merely across the street. Bidding them a good day, he held the door for them to exit the lobby.

Inside the hospital, they stood for a minute to take in their surroundings. The inside looked as one might expect, if they'd ever seen a hospital before. All they had in Paige County was a doctor or two and an old house that was sometimes used to tend to patients who were too contagious to stay at home with family.

The women remarked at how bland the place was. Everything in the hospital was white. The walls were white, the floors were white, and the ceilings were all white. Even the clothes worn by all the staff were white.

"I declare," said Mary Ethel, "a person would surely tire of these bland decorations in no time."

Leola, looking distracted, muttered, "I suppose so."

At the reception desk, a congenial lady about Mary Ethel's age greeted them.

"Good day. May I help you?" asked the woman.

Leola spoke up, "We are here to see Charles Daniel Malone."

"Charles Daniel Malone..." repeated the lady as she ran her finger down a list of names in the registry. "Oh yes, here it is, room number 217. That's on the second floor you know."

"Thank you kindly," replied Leola.

She and Mary Ethel walked to the stairs and began the short climb to the second floor. The stairwell was vacant. The walls were smooth white plaster and hard white tiles covered the floor. Every footstep boomed and echoed so loudly that it was unnerving to them both. When they entered the hallway, they could see CD's room just down from where they were standing.

A rather plump nurse of advanced age was outside his room preparing medicine on a white enameled cart. Leola was relieved to see an older nurse outside his door. To Leola, she did not pose any kind of threat. The two ladies approached and asked about CD.

"Good afternoon," started Leola, "We're here to see Charles Malone. I'm his wife, Leola, and this is his mother, Mary Ethel."

"Oh well, how do you do!" exclaimed the nurse. "We've been anticipating your arrival. Your husband will be thrilled to know you are here. We have just a few things to wrap up for the evening and then you may go in and visit him."

The nurse pointed to a bench down the hall where Mary Ethel and Leola could have a seat, while they waited.

Sitting on the bench, Leola was fidgety. She crossed and uncrossed her legs, shifted from one side to the other, and wrung her hands.

"Child, if you don't sit still and quit your squirmin', you're gonna drive me batty," said Mary Ethel.

"I'm sorry," replied Leola, "I'm just so nervous about seeing Charles."

Mary Ethel patted her knee and encouraged her to take some deep breaths and try to think of calm happy things.

While they were waiting, a young nurse appeared from a doorway and walked in their direction. She was tall and thin. Her hair was sun-kissed. Long blonde curls cascaded like a waterfall over her shoulders, nearly to her waist. Her cheekbones were high and decorated with rouge. She wore blue shadow above her eyes and no wedding ring on her finger. As she passed, she smiled a greeting to Mary Ethel and Leola. Her smile was bright and her teeth were perfect. She was the woman from Leola's fearful imaginings. The beautiful, young nurse was the embodiment of all that Leola feared CD would have chosen over her, had he the chance. She was the most beautiful woman Leola had ever seen.

"Gracious," said Mary Ethel, "That young lady looks like she's right out of the moving picture shows!"

As soon as she passed, she opened the door to CD's room and disappeared inside. Leola's heart sank. She felt a pain in the pit of her stomach—sharp and ancient. It was a familiar ache, the offspring of her tormenting companion—fear. She imagined that CD was inside smiling from ear to ear, at the sight of the beautiful young nurse.

"*I wonder if he even wants to see me?*" she thought to herself.

Leola put her head in her lap and pretended to rest. Mary Ethel had raised five children, had seen some marry, and then have their own. She'd lived long enough to recognize a soul in agony. She did not know the source of Leola's pain exactly, but she knew that someway, somehow, CD was at the center of it.

Mary Ethel rubbed a hand across Leola's back while she prayed silently for the Lord to lift her burden.

After a few minutes, the two nurses came out of CD's room and walked over to the bench where the Malone ladies were seated.

"I think you can see him now," said the older nurse.

Mary Ethel and Leola stood and thanked her. The younger nurse took the opportunity to introduce herself.

"Hello, my name is Alice. I am one of the nurses that has been caring for Mr. Malone," she said.

Mary Ethel spoke for the pair, "I'm Mary Ethel, CD's mother, and this is Leola Malone... his wife."

"Hello," replied Alice, staring at Leola.

For a good long while, Alice carefully studied Leola's face. "*Is everything okay?*" Mary Ethel asked, attempting to break the awkward silence.

The young nurse shook her head, almost embarrassed, and looking at Leola replied, "Yes, of course. I'm sorry, it's just that... it's just that you are as beautiful as Mr. Malone described, even more so."

Her statement caught Leola off guard, "I don't know what you mean."

"Why, you're all Mr. Malone talks about. Nearly every waking moment, he says how much he misses you, how wonderful you are, and what a perfect wife and mother you are. He said you're the most beautiful woman he's ever seen. I hope you don't mind, but he's told us so much about you," replied the nurse smiling.

Leola suppressed a smile and her eyes filled again with tears but this time cleansing, renewing tears. She reached into her clutch and retrieved a small handkerchief. Wiping her eyes, she laughed in relief. The young nurse's words broke something inside of her—something wretched and awful. The kind words spoken by a total stranger pierced deeply into her heart and mortally wounded her tormenting companion. Her long-held fear was at last dying. The feeling was uncomfortable.

"Can we see him now?" asked Leola.

The older nurse replied, "Certainly. Right this way."

As they all walked back down the hallway to CD's room,

Mary Ethel focused on her daughter-in-law. Leola's posture was more erect. Her gate was somehow lighter and for an instant Mary Ethel thought she heard a choir. The moment filled her with joy and happiness for Leola.

"Did CD say anything about me?" she asked jokingly, "After all, I am his mother."

Alice shook her head, and answered, "No ma'am, I'm sorry, he only ever spoke of his wife."

When they reached the door, Alice turned to look at Leola and said, "You know... Mr. Malone said that if he could have his pick of any woman in the whole world, it would be you, every time. You are very blessed. I do hope to find a man so devoted someday."

Leola fairly beamed, "I'm sure you will dear."

When they walked through the door to CD's room, he was sitting up in bed. His leg was no longer in the trapeze, and aside from the obvious, he looked well.

Leola ran to him and exclaimed, "Darling!" She threw her arms around him. Feeling him in her arms set loose a flood of emotions that poured out of her in tears. All of the dread that had built up in her since the morning he'd left Paige County for the city was now gone.

CD held her tight. He squeezed her until he feared she might be injured. "You're all I could think about when I was trapped under that coal car," said CD. "All I wanted was to see you and Pink again."

Looking over Leola's shoulder, he made eye contact with his mother and added, "And you too Mom."

Mary Ethel was wiping tears of joy but managed to mouth the words, "I love you."

CD smiled and released Leola from his embrace.

She looked back at Mary Ethel and beamed. In that moment she knew something dreadful in Leola had been defeated. Leola had been set free.

"I want you to tell me every detail," instructed Leola. "Everyone at the church is praying for you."

CD grinned, "I love you more than anything Leola Reaves Malone and I want you to know that the men I worked with hunted for me all night until I was rescued."

Mary Ethel shared with CD all that the railroad man had told them and about how they were being treated so well.

"There's a man on my crew..." began CD, "there's a man on my crew named Jerome. He's the one who dug me out from under that railcar. He saved my life."

"When can I meet this man and thank him personally?" replied Leola.

CD grinned, "You'll meet him soon enough. We're gonna give him some land to farm."

"Give him some land?" asked Mary Ethel.

"Yep, me and the boys already talked it over, and we're going to carve out thirty acres to give him."

Leola and Mary Ethel looked at each other unsure about what CD was suggesting. The land their family owned had belonged to a Malone, of some sort, for over a hundred years.

Giving away family land just wasn't done, especially to strangers.

"Son, you should get some rest. There will be plenty of time to think about these sorts of things later, after you're on the mend good," replied his mother.

CD looked at Leola and taking her hand he said, "I need to know this is okay with you. Darling, I owe this man my life."

Leola smiled. She saw in her husband's eyes sincerity and the good heart and integrity she had come to appreciate and value.

"I'm sure we'll figure out what is right," she said.

CD looked at Mary Ethel and then back at Leola, "I owe this man my life, and I'm gonna repay him with land!"

Chapter 22

Burnt Biscuits

Doc Weber said it would be at least six weeks before CD's leg would mend completely. The timing of such a serious injury put an enormous strain on him. It was spring, and he already knew he was going to be a little late getting his crops in the ground on account of the temporary job he and his brothers had taken in Charlottesville, but the broken leg made it seem impossible to get everything planted.

In Paige County, people take care of one another. The Malone family was well known for being some of the first to volunteer to help when anyone needed it. So, it naturally followed that the members of the community were more than eager to pitch in to help CD and Leola on their farm.

Word quickly spread throughout the area that CD needed help getting his crops in the ground. People from all over Paige County were eager to lend a hand busting sod and planting corn, cotton, and tobacco. Sheriff Edwards scheduled a meeting after church, one Sunday, to plan the work party over at CD and Leola's farm. On the day of the meeting, nearly 150 people showed up at the church. So many people had turned up to hear how they could help, that Deacon Willie Duncan moved the meeting outside on the church lawn.

Men, women, and children of all ages stood and talked until Pastor Donnie Briscoe began to shout from the front steps of the church to get everyone's attention. The noise from dozens of different conversations made it impossible for many to hear him. He tried yelling again, "May I have your attention please?"

Pastor Donnie looked over at Warner and shrugged. Laughing, Warner reached down and picked up an acorn husk. He placed his thumbs over the top of the husk and blew into the small triangular space between them. The shrill high-pitched whistle jolted everyone in the crowd silent.

Sheriff Edwards put his finger into his ear and wiggled it to alleviate the ringing Warner's makeshift whistle had caused. "Where on earth did you learn to do that?" he asked.

Pleased with himself, Warner smiled and said, "My grandpa showed me how to do that when I was a boy. He said if I got lost, as long as I could find an acorn shell, I'd always have a way to call for help."

Sheriff Edwards thanked him for quieting the crowd and joined the preacher up on the steps.

Pastor Donnie raised his hands and began, "Brothers and sisters, we are indeed thankful that so many have turned out to volunteer to help CD and Leola Malone. It is a true blessing and I know I can speak for the Malones when I say they are most grateful for your willingness to help them during this difficult time. It is fitting that we begin this meeting in prayer, so if you would all join me, let us bow our heads."

As the crowd bowed their heads and the pastor prayed, Pink kept his eyes open and looked around the crowd. He noticed that most people had their eyes closed, but some did not, and some weren't even bowing. He wondered why it was necessary to close his eyes and bow his head in order for his prayers to be heard.

"Maybe it's hard for the Lord to concentrate," he supposed.

The preacher finished up by saying, "...and Lord we are most of all grateful that you have seen fit to return CD Malone to his family and his community in one piece. Give us a spirit of cooperation and diligence in the days forthcoming, so that we might accomplish our noble task, Amen."

When the prayer was over Pastor Donnie called the sheriff up to go over the particulars of how, when, and where everyone was to meet up the following week to turn over the ground and plant for the Malones.

The sheriff explained that he had arranged to borrow a large tent from the next county over, to provide shelter for all the food. Joe and Ed'ard were planning to butcher a steer and roast it for dinner, while ladies from the community were bringing potato salad, biscuits, collards, and of course many varieties of cakes and pies.

"We will all meet at CD's place, next Friday morning at six sharp. Please bring with you anything you will need to work. CD assures me that there will be plenty of water and hay for your mules and horses. I think that about covers it. It's gonna be a long, hard day or two but with your help, we can get this man and his family back on schedule and see to it that they have something come harvest time," he concluded.

As everyone began to return to their homes, Pastor Donnie remarked to Sheriff Edwards that this was the largest crowd they'd ever had at their tiny church.

"Gordy, you're a fine sheriff and a good man," said the preacher.

Gordy smiled and put out his hand to shake. "I'm a better Sheriff, I think, because of the people I get to serve in this county," he replied.

The following morning Pink woke up around the usual time. He lay there in his bed thinking about all that was happening in his family. He was excited for the great many people that would be visiting for the planting on Friday. He'd looked for Charley Aleshire the day before at the meeting but did not see her. Charlotte, or Charley as some called her, had become one of Pink's best friends and he secretly had a crush on her.

After a few minutes, Pink began his morning prayer, "Lord, help me have a good day. I'm gonna try to start gettin' ready for the work party on Friday, so please help me be strong all day, and please work it out, so Charley Aleshire can be here on Friday, Amen."

When Pink went into the kitchen, he was the only person awake. He looked at the clock on the wall and noticed that it was already half past five. He took a couple of biscuits from the pie safe and spread a little apple butter in them. He washed the biscuits down with a glass of water, donned his hat, and slipped quietly out of the door. He was careful not to let the screen door slam, so as not to wake his mother and father. The doctor had made it clear that bed rest and sound sleep were important for his father to heal up.

It was still dark out when he walked off the back porch, so Pink got to work doing what chores he could while he waited for the sun to rise over Hawksbill Mountain. He fed the chickens, mules, and horses and cleaned the stables. After he'd put away the hayfork and shovel, he remembered a bucket of table scraps his mother had saved for the few hogs they kept penned up out in the back of their hay barn.

Pink got the bucket and started off to the hog pen. Every step with the bucket required a deliberate effort to ensure that the contents did not slosh out onto his britches. The stench of the slop in the pale was offensive. Pink wondered how anything could bear to eat it. When he poured the contents of the slop bucket into their trough, the pigs greedily pushed and grunted at one another in an effort to consume as much for themselves as possible.

"Y'all behave now!" Pink hollered, "Nobody likes hateful bacon!"

By the time he'd finished slopping the hogs, the light from the sun was sufficient enough for him to get on with the work he'd planned for the day.

Mules and horses require a lot of water and feed to keep up their strength while they are being worked. Pink knew that at least a dozen families were going to come to their farm to help and that each family would bring animals to pull plows.

To make sure that the animals would be taken care of, he began to set up hay and water stations out where the volunteers from the community would be working on Friday.

From inside the house Leola, now awake, could see Pink working hard. As she made breakfast, she shared with CD that she could see him hauling pails of water to fill a washtub he'd placed out by the fields.

From the bedroom, where he was lying with his leg elevated on a stack of pillows, CD called out, "If that boy makes me any more proud, I'm liable to swell up and bust!"

CD managed to swing his cast off the side of the bed, so that he could sit up. He stretched and yawned rubbing the sleep from his face. He reached for the wooden crutches the doctor had given him and made his way through the door to the kitchen.

"Charles Daniel!" Leola scolded, "Have you so soon forgotten what the doctor told you about bed rest?"

CD smiled and held up one hand as if to signal his surrender, "I swear, I ain't never slept this much in all my life. If I keep this up, I'll be useless by the time this leg mends."

He sat at the table the best he could with his casted leg stretched out resting in the chair across from him. Leola set a cup of coffee down on the table for him and kissed him gently on the lips. She turned to retrieve biscuits from the stove, when CD grabbed her hand to stop her. Leola stiffened, there was something in his touch that felt serious, not playful. She thought she knew what might be on his mind; they had not spoken of the accident since he had been home. Neither CD nor Leola knew how to have such a conversation, but they each knew that what happened down in Charlottesville had changed them both and perhaps their relationship with each other.

For CD, he felt reborn. Under the overturned railroad car, as he drifted in and out of consciousness, he'd experienced more than he could understand or tell. Some good, some bad. His inability to grasp or articulate it made no difference. One thing remained certain in CD's mind— he was a different man.

Leola, too, had experienced a change. Hers was an undoing of a lifetime of fear. She felt free, light, and airy. Her soul felt more like beautifully woven lace than a stone wall—able to breathe. Even though she had always been "happy", *this* happiness was new, deeper, and brighter. Leola was a blushing bride —all smiles—as on the day of her marriage to CD, and when Pink came home to live with them. She'd never felt more fulfilled. Still, this new feeling that had surprised her so quickly and overwhelmed her so thoroughly, was both foreign and welcomed. She struggled to name this feeling but suspected it might be joy. Joy, true and honest joy, without strings or conditions. Joy without expectation, doubt, or fear... just honest to goodness, down deep in her soul, joy... and it felt wonderful.

CD held his grip on her hand, gently but resolutely—Leola turned and knelt beside his chair. CD looked into her eyes and there professed his love.

"I loved you the moment I saw you. I love you when I'm awake, when I am sleeping, and I will love you as long as I live," CD paused to collect himself. Tears welled up in his eyes and he continued, "I expect I will love you even after I am dead, if it's possible."

"I love you too," she replied. She smiled a smile that CD had seen before but infrequently. A smile that came from a place of happiness, true joy, and belonging.

"I remember the day you asked me to marry you," said Leola. "You were as nervous as a long-tailed housecat in a room full of rocking chairs."

CD grinned, "It was all I could do to remember my own name in that moment, I almost forgot to give you the flowers I'd picked."

Leola, placing a hand on CD's cheek, replied, "They were beautiful and fresh. I can still smell... THE BISCUITS!" Leola jumped up and yanked open the door to the stove. Great clouds of smoke billowed from the oven as she reached inside with a mitt and retrieved a dozen blackened cinders that were meant to be biscuits.

She and CD were laughing hysterically. The burning of biscuits in that household had become somewhat of a tradition. As she opened the window to let the smoke out from the charred bread, she could see Pink steadily working, hauling pails of water.

Throwing the burnt biscuits out of the window, she shouted at Pink to dowse the smoking biscuits with water. Pink ran over to the kitchen window, all the while sloshing water from the pail onto his britches. By the time he reached the house, there was barely a quarter pail of water left.

Emptying the pail onto the smoldering cinders Pink asked, "What happened?"

"I burned the biscuits," she laughed.

Pink smiled and replied, "They look like lumps of coal.

Maybe I'll save 'em and give them to that mean old Butch Cole for Christmas next year."

"Oh, you be nice," chided his mother.

Pink chuckled and returned to his work while Leola returned to her "darling Charles."

While Pink worked outside, Leola and CD sat together at the kitchen table, talking and laughing for the entire morning. It had been years since the two of them had carried on so. CD reminded her of the first time he'd kissed her at 'Dinner on the Lawn' behind the church.

"I still can't believe you kissed me at church!" she said. "I was terrified that my mother and father would find out."

CD grinned, "I'd have kissed you in front of the preacher and the whole church that day, if I could have!"

Leola looked into his eyes and pushed his hair back away from his face. She hesitated to say what she wanted to tell him. She believed it now, but somehow saying it out loud seemed dangerous to her. For the first time in their marriage, Leola knew, without a doubt, that CD loved her and would have chosen her over any other woman in the world. She'd come to see herself differently too. She no longer believed that she was unworthy of his love. Leola now saw herself, the way her husband did, as a beautiful, talented, and kind woman.

So much of what Leola believed about herself had changed since the accident. As she allowed one of her greatest fears to come out of the shadows and into the light, her fear gave way to love. Leola had found the free space she needed to finally see CD's undying love and devotion shining like a beacon in her heart. She now knew that she not only deserved his adoration, but that CD himself was lucky to be married to her. All those years ago, CD has chosen Leola as his one and only. At the hospital, Leola had finally chosen to believe and abide in that love, so much so that it had now become her inner truth.

Often, inner truths are easier to believe in secret than to share with others. Saying it out loud removes the possibility of going back. In her mind, she had composed several ways to say it and then just decided to simply blurt it out.

"Charles, there isn't another woman in the whole wide world who could make you happy or love you the way that I do, and you are the luckiest man alive to be married to me," she stated abruptly.

CD grinned with a look of surprise on his face. He pulled his head back and looked at her in admiration.

"I know that," he replied incredulously, and then he added, "But it makes my heart happy to hear you say it."

"When they told me you had been injured, I never doubted that you would be okay," said Leola, "But I had feared you would fall in love with someone else, while you were away in the city."

CD took her face in his hands and replied, "Never, never in all the years, from the day I first saw you, until the end of time, will I love another."

All morning, the two of them drank coffee and talked. Their conversation was free, honest, and open. Leola found herself sharing her heart freely with CD—all the things that she'd feared, as well as all the things she still dreamed of for their family.

It was a morning of healing and renewal.

"I declare," said CD, "I don't think I have ever enjoyed a conversation as much in all my life!"

Leola smiled, and simply replied, "Me too."

Just then, someone knocked on the back porch door.

CD surmised that it was probably Doc Weber coming to check up on him, so Leola got up to see who it was.

"Well, good morning," greeted Leola. "Come in."

Warner and Mary Ethel stepped inside and took off their coats, hanging them on pegs by the window.

With a quizzical look on her face, Mary Ethel asked, "Leola dear, did you know there are a good dozen or so biscuits on the ground under your kitchen window that look more akin to lumps of coal?"

"Yes ma'am," replied Leola, almost laughing, "I know."

Mary Ethel smiled shaking her head and let the matter drop.

"Who is it?" shouted CD from the kitchen.

Mary Ethel put her finger over her mouth to signal Leola not to answer. She walked to the doorway and could see her son sitting in a chair—not resting in bed.

"Young man, what did the doctor tell you about staying in the bed?" scolded Mary Ethel.

Craning his neck around to see her, CD answered, "Leola said it was okay."

Laughing; Leola, Mary Ethel, and Warner sat down at the table and began to visit.

When Friday came around, eighty members of the community arrived at CD and Leola's farm. There were a dozen plows, with horses and mules to draw them, and Horace Yoder even drove his Fordson tractor all the way from his place, just so he could help. Some of the families, who came to help, had travelled hours to get there with their wagons, plows, and work animals.

So many people came to lend a hand, and not just with the crops. Folks, young and old, came to help prepare meals, tend to the animals, and fetch water out to the men who were working in the fields.

To Pink's great delight, Charlotte Aleshire's family showed up to help, and she and Pink palled around the entire time. And as these things go...Pink fell in love that weekend.

In just two days, ninety-five acres of corn, cotton, and tobacco went into the ground. In due course, CD's leg mended well enough and in time for lay-by and eventually the harvest.

The logistics of what took place at CD and Leola's farm was a feat talked about all the way to Richmond! Sheriff Edwards was even interviewed over the telephone for the newspaper in Charlottesville. He told the newsman that he'd never been so proud of the people of Paige County.

Chapter 23

I Didn't Mean To

"That sure was a mighty fine breakfast mama!" exclaimed Pink. "You make the best flapjacks in the whole county, dirt-n-all!"

Leola smiled at her boy. She'd dreamed of having children since she could remember and when Pink came along, she felt as though an eternal purpose in her had been fulfilled. It made her heart feel good to hear that he'd enjoyed his breakfast.

"I'm glad you liked them. They should give you plenty of energy to get your chores done before your daddy gets home from the mill. I think there might even be time to find a fish or two in Uncle Jim's pond later this evening, if you hustle and get your work done," replied Leola.

"Yes, ma'am," answered Pink.

After wiping off the last traces of molasses and licking it from his finger, Pink stood up and put his plate in the sink.

Finishing his cup of buttermilk, he placed it in the sink with the plate and fork and kissed his mother on the cheek.

It was the spring of 1923, Pink was twelve-years-old and a big help to his pa around the farm. At a little past seven in the morning the high humidity was already causing it to feel extremely hot, or what folks in Paige County called, "stifling".

Pink walked out onto the back porch and noticed that he'd left his homemade bow and arrow set hanging on a branch in the pear tree near the edge of the pasture. He'd been practicing his aim the day before; shooting arrow, after homemade arrow, into a stack of hay bales.

Pink's bow was made from a piece of green ash with a strip of rawhide glued onto the front along its full length. When his granddaddy Warner had helped him make it, he'd explained that the rawhide would make it stronger and springier.

The arrows for his set were just reeds that Pink had sharpened on one end and hardened over a flame in the wood stove, while the fletching at the back of the arrows were just chicken feathers. Pink would choose the straightest reeds he could find, split one end, and then insert a chicken feather to give the arrow some semblance of stable flight. Up close, Pink was fairly accurate with his archery setup but at long distances, the arrows flew like drunken crows, his daddy would say. Still, it was fun to shoot them way up in the sky to see how far they would go.

When he stepped down off the porch, he spied Sampson. Sampson was a Brown Leghorn rooster and the prize bird in his daddy's flock. Sampson was a big rooster and mean. Beautifully colored, he had a burnt orange neck, a green and black breast, blue and orange wings, and long curved tail feathers that were green, blue, and orange. Ol' Sampson was a handsome bird all right, but all that was just a pretty facade. Under that colorful plumage was a spiteful, territorial, and dangerous piece of poultry.

Pink's mom and daddy had only ever heard him swear once. It was on one of the many occasions when Sampson had chased him around the yard, only this particular time the old rooster had caught up to Pink and spurred him good all over his leg.

The spikes on the rooster's legs were long and sharp and the bird knew how to use them. In fact, that old rooster had once successfully fended off a red fox after it had gotten into the chicken pen.

Pink hated that rooster like the devil hates holy water. He was a formidable foe and many times Pink had wished him dead. The problem was that the rooster was important to the chicken flock, and he happened to be his daddy's favorite rooster.

As he stared at the rooster, Pink thought about how much he hated him. Sampson was over by the tool shed where the garden hoes, hayforks, and other tools were kept.

Unfortunately, Pink needed a garden hoe to get his weeding done and that mean old yard-buzzard was in his way. Not sure what to do, Pink picked up a handful of small gravel and threw it at the rooster, sending him scurrying off.

Satisfied that the threat was gone, Pink walked over to the

tool shed and opened the door. It was dark inside but the light coming in from the door was enough for him to pick out the hoe he wanted. Since he was working by himself, he had his choice. There was one that had been in the family for so long that its blade was almost as thin as a butter knife. The narrow blade made it easier to reach under the plants. The handle had spent so much time in the hands of various Malone's over the years that it was as smooth as silk. The oil and sweat from Pink's father, mother, grandfather, great-grandfather, and so on had cured and broken in the handle until it had become the family favorite.

When Pink walked out of the tool shed, that confounded chicken was waiting for him and chased him all the way out by the pasture. It was almost more than Pink could do; to resist beating Sampson to death with the hoe. He screamed and yelled at the rooster as he zigzagged back and forth running as fast as he could.

When the rooster finally lost interest in chasing Pink, he turned around and strutted back to the chicken coup.

"Get on outta here! You sock-eyed mule!" hollered Pink.

He walked out to the garden but stopped by the pear tree to fetch his bow and arrow set. He wanted to be prepared in the event that any wild animals attacked or if some marauding road bandits happened by their place. In young Pink's mind, there was always danger lurking and he wanted to be prepared, in case there was trouble afoot.

When he got to the garden, he began the job of chopping the weeds from around the different vegetable plants that had already come up. It was late in May and the garden was looking swell. The Kentucky Wonder pole beans were already long enough to train on the cotton-twine trellises, tomato plants had green fruit, collards were up, and the yellow squash plants were in bloom.

Pink loved the family garden. He especially enjoyed the popcorn they grew. Precious few things came out of their garden that Pink didn't like—except beets. He hated beets. He didn't hate them enough to sabotage the crop but enough to negotiate extra chores in exchange for not having to eat them.

Having a reasonably good time with his work, Pink was whistling a tune his granddaddy Warner had taught him. Thinking back, Pink could remember the first time he heard his granddaddy whistling the song.

"*What's that one grandpa?" asked Pink.*

"*Oh, it's just an old tune I heard from my daddy years ago, after he got back from the war.*"

"*Which war was that one?" asked Pink.*

Your great-granddaddy was in the War between the States," he replied.

"*The Civil War?" asked Pink.*

"*Yep, that's the one," Warner answered.*

"*What's the name of it?" asked Pink. His curiosity was piqued and his grandfather knew the only way to satisfy the boy's query was to answer him outright.*

"*Well, it's called the 'Battle Hymn of the Republic'. It's the song them Yankee boys sang marchin' into battle," answered his grandpa.*

"But I wouldn't go around whistling it too much around these folks here though," he added with a wink.

"Oh, well it sure is catchy," replied Pink.

That was all Pink said about the song. He'd never understood the fixation some in the valley had about the Civil War. To his young mind, the war was over, the matter decided, and there was no need to discuss it further, save to never repeat the atrocity itself.

Out in the garden under the bright sun, it wasn't long before he'd taken off his shirt. Pink worked and sweated as hard as a grown man, only taking breaks to drink water from his genuine US Army canteen that his Uncle Edward had brought back from the Great War.

Finishing the last row of corn, Pink looked back and admired his work. *"Daddy'll be proud,"* he thought. He turned up the canteen and drank the remaining water. When he put it down, he looked in the direction of the barn, and he saw *that* rooster—and he hated him.

Pink picked up his bow and aimed an arrow in the direction of the rooster. Sampson was at least a hundred and fifty feet away, so there was no danger that the arrow would actually hit the chicken from that distance—or so he thought.

Pink launched the arrow high as if he were aiming at the sun. Pulling back the string, as far the arrow would permit, he let it fly. The crooked shaft, made from a reed, zigzagged in the air back and forth and up and down. When the arrow reached its apex, it nosed over and began a rapid descent.

Watching the arrow travel toward the rooster, Pink was

impressed with his aim. The arrow was getting closer to the chicken than he ever thought possible.

"That's not a bad shot," he thought to himself.

Suddenly—disaster! Just before it reached the ground, the arrow curved to one side and shot straight through the old rooster's head. Pink panicked and ran as fast as he could to catch Sampson, who was now flailing his wings and squawking loudly, but the chicken was too far away and too fast.

Sampson disappeared under the barn, way back into the crawl space, where it was too dark for Pink to see. He could hear the rooster making a fuss but could not see him. After a while, the noise stopped and Pink knew the rooster had succumbed to his injuries.

His lifelong struggle to adapt to being loved and accepted made moments like this one extraordinarily terrifying. Despite the unconditional love his family poured over him, there was sometimes a nagging voice whispering the lie, "It's not true, mess up and they'll abandon you."

He began to pray. "Dear Lord, I've killed Daddy's prize rooster and I don't know what to do. Please, please help me find that bird and bury him before Daddy gets home and finds out what I done. I don't want to have to go away from here. Amen."

Now, Granddaddy Warner used to say that all prayers get an answer. Sometimes the Lord says, "Yes." sometimes "No." and sometimes "Not yet."

On this particular day, it was a clear "NO!"

After a couple of hours of trying to see under the barn, reach under with a cane pole, and summon the courage to crawl under the barn with all the snakes, spiders, and every other horrible creature a twelve-year-old boy can imagine, Pink gave up. He accepted the fact that he was just going to have to tell his daddy what he'd done. So he went back to work, finishing up his chores.

When his father got home, Pink helped him unload the cornmeal from the mill, while he recounted all the chores he'd gotten done while his daddy had been gone.

At supper, CD asked Pink if he knew where the rooster was. "I didn't see Sampson when I fed the chickens and penned them up for the night. Did you see him today, Son?" asked CD.

"Yes, sir," replied Pink, "Last time I saw him, he was over by the pasture huntin' up worms and bugs and mess to eat."

"Hmmm," replied his daddy, "I sure hope he didn't wander off or get eaten by that fox."

Pink kept silent. He hadn't lied to his daddy... *well...* not outright anyway, so he decided to keep his mouth shut and not chance it.

After supper, CD and Pink went outside to put away a few hand tools that were still out by the plow shed. Pink went out of the door first; as soon as he stepped off the back porch, he exclaimed, "Oh no!"

Pink's hound dog, Rufus, was draggin' that dead rooster around the yard, and what's worse is that Pink's arrow was still sticking through its head.

"What in the world!" yelled CD.

The sight left CD flabbergasted. He didn't have to ask what

had happened to poor Sampson—the evidence was protruding from each side of the demised chicken's head.

"Daddy, I'm real sorry!" shouted Pink. As long buried memories allowed fear to touch his heart, Pink burst into tears. And before he could think to run, CD grabbed him up and embraced him in a deep hug. When Pink finally relaxed and calmed down enough to talk, CD gently released him.

He sat Pink down on the edge of the porch, and gave him a chance to come clean about the dead chicken. The remorseful boy told his daddy every gory detail. He told him about Sampson chasing him around the yard that morning and how he'd shot the arrow from so far away, he didn't think it would even come close, let alone kill the chicken. And then he explained how Sampson had scurried under the barn, but he was too afraid to crawl under there to get him for the stew pot.

"I didn't mean to kill him," explained a heartfelt Pink.

CD shook his head and replied, "Well, you didn't mean not to." CD explained that that if Pink had never fired the arrow in the first place, the rooster would still be alive. "Son, you have wasted a good rooster. Besides killing breeding stock, the meat has spoiled because you didn't fetch him out from under that barn."

All the commotion raised Leola's curiosity, and she came out on the porch to see what all the fuss was about. "Is everything alright out here?" she asked.

CD looked at Pink and said, "Go on... tell your mama what you've done."

Pink explained again, in great detail, what had happened to the rooster. When he'd finished the story, Leola looked at the dead rooster, the arrow through its head, and the hound dog that was busy figuring out how to eat it, and said, "Good. It's high time somebody killed that hateful bird." And without another word, she turned around and went back in the house.

CD and Pink both burst into raucous laughter.

Chapter 24

A Live Standin' Up Cow

The school hack turned down the dirt road that led to the adjacent farms that Pink and 'Lij's families lived on. The road was washed out and rutted. There was no shortage of bumps and jostles on the hack when it was on the good road, but the Malone road was nearly intolerable.

"Great day in the morning!" shouted the driver. "You boys tell your daddies to hit a lick on this road. I swear to heaven above; my teeth are gonna rattle outta my head."

'Lij looked at his cousin and grinned. "If it weren't for that hide glue, his teeth woulda fallen out a long time ago," he said.

Pink was already laughing before he'd finished the sentence. "You better stop it. If he tells your daddy on you, you'll be in a heap of trouble," he chided.

Attempting to change the subject before their laughter caused them grief, Pink asked, "What chores do you have when you get home?"

Elijah smiled hopefully and replied, "I gotta barn two cows, milk 'em and then bring in the night's stove wood is all," he said. "Why? What do you figure on doing this evening?"

"Well, Uncle Jim told me that the crappie are starting to bite close to the bank at his pond and I thought we might go try to catch a mess to eat," replied Pink. Continuing he added, "I ain't got but a couple of chores myself, and I just found me a new fishin' pole on the creek and I want to try it out."

"You found a fishin' pole? What kind of fishin' pole?" asked 'Lij.

Pink began to whisper, "I was traipsin' on Hawksbill Creek Sunday afternoon, and I spied a real nice cane pole in the brush. It looks store-bought. Not like them ones we make from reeds," he explained.

"And you just took it?" asked 'Lij. There was a bit of shock in Elijah's tone.

"Well, yeah, I mean it was just layin' there in the bushes. It's not like I took it from Floyd's or anything." Pink sounded almost defensive.

Elijah replied, "Okay, I guess that's alright." Still, he wasn't sure.

The pair sat in silence for a while longer until the school hack made its way up the hill toward the Malone's end of the road. Looking out into the pasture beside Pink's house, Elijah could see Gerty. She was a wide-hipped milk cow. She was the only thing living on that place that gave any milk. The cow was a Guernsey and had a mean spirit about her, or so thought Pink. It is more likely though, that the cow's only crime was her preference for the fresh dry hay in the barn rather than being staked out on a chain, all day in the pasture.

"I can't stand that stupid animal!" said Pink. "I'd rather drink kerosene and pee on a brushfire than to mess with her one more time!"

Elijah grinned. His cousin's disdain for something as simple as an old milk cow amused him. He also enjoyed watching Pink fight the cow to keep her under control every day.

"You lead that cow back to the barn every day, Pink. You outta figure out a way to break her of runnin' off like that," offered Elijah. "I don't know how you've been able to stand it this long. Every day that cow bolts to the barn and drags that old rusty chain through your hands."

Pink looked at 'Lij and thought for a moment. He rubbed his hand across his chin. Elijah could see the wheels turning in Pink's head.

"You better be careful thinkin' that hard. I can smell the sawdust in your head burnin'," said 'Lij.

"Ha-ha," said Pink with a smirk. "I think I know exactly what I'm gonna do," he said.

"Oh yeah, what?" replied 'Lij.

Pink did not answer, but nodded his head confidently. In his mind, he had solved the problem; regrettably, there's no way Pink could've possibly known, just how dramatically his life was about to change. In one's lifetime, every person should learn to look beyond the impulse of a single moment and carefully consider the long-lasting consequences of one's ill-considered actions.

Pink had not.

"What's your big plan, Pink?" asked Elijah.

"Never you mind," answered Pink. "I'm gonna break Gerty of suckin' eggs and tearin' up my hands with that old chain."

When the hack stopped, 'Lij and Pink hopped out and Elijah started up the path to his house.

Pink, on the other hand, walked out into the pasture where the cow was staked. Immediately, the cow stopped grazing and walked toward the barn as far as the chain would permit. She was already anticipating the dry hay and warm stall of the barn. It was her daily routine, but all that was about to change.

Pink knelt on one knee, poised to jump to his feet as quickly as possible. He slowly unscrewed the clevis that attached the chain to the stake, never taking his eye off of Gerty. "This is it, you stupid cow," whispered Pink. "Today you'll learn better than to run off from me."

Unscrewing the pin in the clevis was not easy, as the cow was already straining against the chain, making it almost impossible to turn the screw. Pink jerked at the chain and the cow gave up some slack. She turned to look at him, as if to say, "Are you ready to race?"

"Just hold on a minute!" shouted Pink. The wheels were in motion in his head. His disgust and anger had a better hold on him right then than good judgment. Pink pulled at the chain gently until he had most of the slack in his hand. As he reeled her in, Gerty walked gently but reluctantly back toward Pink and the stake. Once satisfied that he had enough chain in his hand, he released the clevis and let it fall on the ground.

When the clevis hit the ground, it rang like a bell. Gerty knew the sound meant the chain was off the stake, and the race was on. She bolted to a gallop and a good ten feet of the chain slipped through Pink's hand like a saw.

"Oww!!" he screamed. "You confounded milk bag! You got it coming!"

Pink sprinted with all his might to catch up to and pass the cow. He got about fifteen feet in front of her and just like he'd planned, he wrapped the chain around the trunk of an old pear tree that was growing at the edge of the pasture. Pink squatted on the ground, next to the tree, and held the chain tight so it could not unwrap itself.

Gerty never let up. She was doing what she'd always done and Pink's strange antics had made no difference to her until...

Until the chain got taut.

When Gerty had run all the slack out of the chain, it snapped tight and jerked her head to a violent stop, which propelled her body out in front of her and up into the air. She landed on the ground with a great thud.

"Yaaaaaaaa hoooooo!" Pink let out a victory cry. But the celebration was short-lived, as Pink noticed that Gerty wasn't moving or getting up.

"*Holy smokes!*" he thought. "*I've done killed the only milk cow we got.*"

Just then, he could hear Elijah calling out from down the path to his house. He was running toward Pink and the deceased milk cow at a good clip.

"Good Lord Almighty! You killed Gerty! You killed Gerty!"
he shouted stumbling over his feet.

Breathless and sweating, 'Lij finally got over to the pear tree
where Pink was now pacing and kicking rocks.

"Daddy'll be mad as hornets for sure. What'll I do?"
pleaded Pink.

"You gotta get outta here," exclaimed 'Lij. "You better pack
yourself a poke and hit the road."

"I ain't got no place to go," replied a panicked Pink. "Where
should I go?"

'Lij thought for a moment and offered a solution, "You pack
yourself some clothes and a few biscuits out of the pie safe and
you get to Granddaddy Warner and Grandma Mary Ethel's as
fast as you can."

"Good idea. Yeah, that's what I'll do," replied Pink.

"Grandma and Grandpa will know what to do," assured 'Lij.

The pair ran as fast as they could to Pink's house. Bursting
through the door Pink called out, "'Lij, get me some biscuits
from the pie safe and a slice of cornbread, if there's any."

Elijah hollered back, "Okay!"

Pink raced to the back of the house and slipped the case off
his pillow and filled it with socks, a change of under-drawers
and a clean shirt. He ran back to the kitchen where Elijah was
waiting with some bread wrapped in a kerchief.

"Hold the pillowcase open," 'Lij instructed.

'Lij dropped the handkerchief into the pillowcase and Pink
twisted it shut and tossed it over his shoulder.

'Lij put out his hand and said, "It's been damned fine
knowin' you."

"I ain't dying or goin' away for good!" said Pink incredulously. "I'm just going to Grandma and Grandpa's for a few days. And don't swear!"

'Lij came to himself, looked embarrassed, and said, "Oh yeah, right. Well, I sure hope your pa ain't too mad when he finds out you killed that cow."

"I sure didn't mean to kill her," mourned Pink.

'Lij put his arm around Pink's shoulder as they walked out to the back porch.

As they stepped down into the yard, 'Lij pointed his finger and hollered, "Looky yonder!"

Pink looked in the direction he was pointing, and there by the pear tree was Gerty grazing on the grass under the tree. The chain was still attached to the tree trunk and the cow was still attached to the chain.

The cow looked a little wobbly—but she was standing up!

Pink began to cry. The tension that had built up inside him was too great to hold and the dam finally burst. He sobbed so much, he fell down on his knees with his face in his hands.

"What are you crying about? Gerty's alive and you ain't gotta run away now!" said 'Lij.

"I ain't sad," said Pink. "It's just that I've never been so happy to see a live standin' up cow.

Chapter 25

A Bonafide Malone Man

"Give me a hand with this yoke," said Warner. Ed'ard did his best to hold the mule steady, while Warner and CD picked up the yoke and tried to slip it over the animal's head.

The mule pushed backward and knocked Ed'ard to the ground. CD yanked hard on the harness to try and control the ornery creature.

"Whoa, don't do that!" admonished Warner, "You'll just make him mad."

CD looked perplexed and straining to hold the mule's head down, replied, "He seems pretty mad already, Daddy!"

"Boy, this mule ain't even got a good start on mad yet. I've seen this mule, right here, fight off four grown men and send 'em off limpin'," Warner contended.

"Well," said Ed'ard sarcastically, "It's a good thing there's three of us."

Warner and two of his sons were over at Uncle Jim's place

attempting to help him get last season's vegetable garden plowed under, but the resident old mule was what folks around there called, "used up". It wasn't that the animal was mean, or old, or stupid, it was that he was all three and quite strong to boot.

The trio fought the mule for about ten minutes more and finally managed to get him hooked up to the cultivator.

After the mule finally accepted that the only way back out to the pasture and his customarily easy life was to finish the job of turning under the remnants of Jim's vegetable garden, he settled down and worked as easily as any mule could be expected.

While CD commenced to plowing, Warner and Ed'ard joined Jim on the back porch and sipped a taste of Jim's home-made whiskey to pass the time.

"This sure is a fine batch, brother," said Warner. "I reckon this might be the best you ever made."

"Naw, it ain't the best. I made a batch last month that was a whole lot better than this," replied Jim.

Ed'ard was watching CD make a turn with the mule and the cultivator when he heard Jim say there was a better batch of shine than the one they were drinking. He turned to look at his Uncle, and smiling big, exclaimed, "Well, let's have a taste of that one!"

Jim shook his head and said, "Sorry boys, I done drank all that up."

Warner stopped his rocking chair and sat up straight. He looked at Ed'ard to see his reaction, and it was the same as his —shock.

"You drank it all?" exclaimed Warner.

"Yep," replied Jim

"All of it?" Ed'ard asked in disbelief.

Jim was now wishing he hadn't mentioned the batch of moonshine he'd polished off all by himself, but it was too late, that horse had left the barn and there weren't no callin' it back.

"I reckon that's why y'all ain't seen me at the church for a few weeks... I ain't been sober enough to get there," Jim confessed.

Warner and Ed'ard began to laugh so loud that CD stopped the mule and hollered from the garden, "What's so all-fired funny?"

"Get back to work, we'll tell you later," yelled Ed'ard in reply.

CD shook his head and gave the reins a snap to send the mule back to a steady pull. After a half hour more, CD made the final pass to till under Uncle Jim's garden and guided the mule over to the plow shed.

Noticing that CD had finished up, Warner and Ed'ard got down off the porch and walked out to the barn grove to help CD with the cultivator and the tack.

Turning toward his Uncle Jim, who was still sitting on the porch, CD yelled, "Where's your saddle soap?"

"Don't worry about all that CD, I'll do it later," answered Jim.

Warner and his sons fed and watered the mule and then let him in the gate to the pasture. The mule trotted straight away to a bare spot and began to wallow in the dust.

"When you boys were little I could have sworn that's what

you must have been doin' all day," said Warner. "Your mama used to say that you boys could muddy up bathwater with one foot."

Ed'ard and CD laughed, and the three of them walked back up to the house.

As they approached, Warner could see Pink and 'Lij coming up the path, from the good road, totin' their fishin' poles. The pair were singing something, but they were murdering the tune so thoroughly that no one could tell what song it was. As they drew near the house, it became clear that they were singin' a poem Mary Ethel had taught Pink when he was a little boy. "Fishy, Fishy in the brook, daddy caught him with a hook, mama fried him in the pan, and baby ate him like a man."

"I remember that one," said Ed'ard. CD nodded his head in agreement.

The poem was one of dozens that Mary Ethel could recite from memory. She had always taught her children, and now grandchildren, little things to memorize. "Building a strong memory, builds a strong mind and memorizing the right things, builds a strong character," she would often say.

Pink and 'Lij reached the porch where Uncle Jim, Grand-daddy Warner, Uncle Ed'ard, and Pink's daddy were sitting. They were already grinning and plotting ways to give the two boys a good measure of grief when they came within earshot. It wasn't because the boys had done anything wrong (*that they knew of*) but young boys need to be given grief to help them learn to spar with their wits and not only their fists. It was the way of things in Paige County, at least. One might suspect that it is the same everywhere, always has been, and always should be.

"You boys look like you each need a parvo shot," called out Uncle Jim. "If'n I had a mule that was as scrawny as you boys, I'd have used him for catfish bait a long time ago."

'Lij knew Uncle Jim was just crackin' their corn, but he also knew a reply was expected. He took another step, pausing to think.

"C'mon son, you're stalling," said Uncle Ed'ard. "Your daddy's taught you better than to take it lyin' down."

Starting from a very young age, the young boys in the Malone family had to learn to walk a fine line—how to respond in the sparring of words with their elders without venturing into disrespect. Pink thought of a really good retort, but it wasn't his turn as he had not been addressed directly.

'Lij stood silent at the bottom of the porch steps, while all the men smiled big that he'd been caught flat and had no response. As they exchanged satisfied glances, Uncle Jim spoke up.

"I guess that about does it," Uncle Jim said, laughing a good-hearted laugh. "Don't worry, there will be plenty of opportunities for you, especially in this family...unless you want to give it a try Pink?" he continued.

Without a second to even draw a full breath, Pink blurted, "Well, if we could grow big and strong by flappin' our gums, I reckon we'd be seventy-some years old and rockin' on the back porch by now."

All of the men burst into laughter. Warner looked over at

Jim, now red-faced trying to catch his breath, and said, "I 'spect that might be the best one I've heard in a while. And right on the money."

Elijah slid his boot over and tapped Pink's shoe. He gave Pink a look of gratitude. He'd bested Uncle Jim, at a game people said went back in the Malone family as far as creation.

Pink felt fully grown again and capable. He felt acceptance, and more than that— love. These were feelings that did not come to him often, and when they did, they fled from him as quickly as they'd come. To Pink, his whole existence in the Malone family felt at times precarious and probationary. Persistent whispers that he would never be a real Malone plagued him always, but in that moment, he *was* a Malone man. Bonafide!

Warner caught his breath from the laughter and smiled at Pink, and he could feel his grandfather's pride. It gave him something he could not name. His grandfather's approval had always given Pink something that he could barely describe, let alone assign a name. But he knew how it made him feel. It was a lifeline and more—an anchor. With a simple pat on the back or an approving smile, his grandfather could baptize his soul in light.

After the laughter subsided and everyone settled down, Uncle Jim, still grinning, offered the boys a seat on the porch and a taste of the whiskey.

"Boys," Uncle Jim said, holding out a jar of the shine, "This here will put hair on your chest thick enough to fool a bear into thinking you're his kin."

Pink reached for the jar and pretended to take a swig.

Turning up the jar, he kept his lips pinched shut. When he finished, he wiped his mouth on his shirt sleeve and let out a harsh gasp and a loud sigh, just as he'd seen the other men do.

He held the jar out to Elijah, but he politely declined.

"I better hold off. I got chores later," said 'Lij.

Pink nodded at 'Lij, and he could tell that his cousin knew he hadn't really sipped any of the whiskey. Elijah shot him a wink to let him know his secret was safe.

Uncle Jim turned his attention back to Elijah and Pink. They had shown up with their cane poles and a coffee can full of earthworms.

"If you boys are lookin' for a fish or two, you might be in luck," said Uncle Jim. "Last Saturday, those Harris boys caught a five-quart pail full of bream. They left me a few for my supper and I tell you, they had more fish roe in 'em than I think I've ever seen," he added.

Chapter 26

Rats, Corn, and Gasoline

'Lij and Pink looked at each other and smiled. More than anything, those two loved to go fishing. Earlier that summer, Pink caught a bass out of Uncle Jim's pond that he said was the biggest one ever caught there. More than just the activity of catching fish, they both loved being outdoors and together. Elijah was Pink's best friend in the whole world. Friends are hard to come by, and the kind of friend 'Lij was to Pink, is almost as rare as hen's teeth.

After a good while, CD walked down to the small lake where Pink and 'Lij were fishing. As he approached the two cousins, he could hear them laughing and cuttin' up. 'Lij was telling Pink something about a girl he had a crush on, and Pink was chiding him about her talking him into getting married.

"I believe both of you are too young to think about marriage," said CD. "Best you concentrate on your schoolin' for now and getting' all your chores done."

Pink and 'Lij whirled around to see CD walking up behind them. 'Lij had an embarrassed look on his face.

"We ain't thinkin' about gettin' married, Uncle CD," said 'Lij. "We're just shootin' the breeze."

CD laughed and sat down on the bank of the lake and pulled the stringer of fish up to inspect the catch. There were about a dozen fish on the line.

There was one good-sized bass, a few bream, and a half dozen giant crappie. CD gave the boys a nod of approval and slipped the stringer back into the water.

"Well boys, I have a chore for you to get done for me this afternoon, if you don't mind," said CD.

"What is it Daddy?" asked Pink.

"The rats have nearly taken over at the mule barn and I need you boys to get rid of them for me," answered CD. "If we don't keep the rat population down, we'll all end up with the typhus," he added. "Pink, you boys get home and give those fish to your mama and she'll see to 'em. Then I want you to go in the shed by the mule barn and get that new box of rat poison and dump a little of it down every rat hole you can find."

"Yes, sir," replied Pink. The two boys gathered up their fishing poles, the creel of fish, and started home. It was about a thirty-minute walk to get to Pink's house from Uncle Jim's place, so the pair wrapped the fish in wet burlap to keep them from spoiling in the heat.

When the two cousins arrived back at Pink's house, they hung the stringer of fish on a nail on one of the back porch posts.

Pink's mother was digging in the vegetable garden

scratching up some potatoes for supper. Pink and 'Lij walked over to the edge of the garden to tell her about their catch.

Leola saw the boys hang up the fish and as they approached, she commented about the potatoes. "These are the deepest growing taters I've ever seen. I almost need a shovel instead of a potato rake."

"Mama," Pink began, "Daddy said we're to give you the fish we caught at Uncle Jim's lake and then go poison the rats at the mule barn."

Leola stopped and leaning on the hoe and with a concerned look said, "I don't like you messin' with that poison. I think it's dangerous. If it'll kill rats, it can't be good for folks."

"We'll be careful Aunt Leola," said Elijah.

"Well, be sure you are," she replied.

"Yes ma'am," answered the boys in unison and they headed off to the mule barn.

"You know, I bet we could find a way to get rid of them rats without even touching that poison powder," said Pink.

"Oh, yeah. How do you mean?" asked Elijah.

Pink grinned a grin that 'Lij had seen many times. Elijah knew that grin usually meant that they were about to get into some sort of trouble.

"What if we just put a little gasoline down every hole and burn 'em out?" suggested Pink.

"Sound's dangerous," said 'Lij.

"Naw," replied Pink, "It'll be fine. If the fire is under the ground in the rat tunnels, it can't possibly catch anything else on fire— but it'll kill all the rats."

"I don't know about that," said 'Lij.

"Oh, come on," said Pink, "Are you chicken?"

"I ain't chicken!" exclaimed 'Lij.

"Alright then, go fetch me that 10-quart can of gasoline from the car shed," ordered Pink.

Elijah complied and shortly returned with a small metal can filled with gasoline. Pink was waiting with a makeshift torch made from a stick and a few strips of old cloth wrapped around the end.

Pink and 'Lij very carefully poured a small amount of gasoline down every rat hole they could find. Then, after each pouring, they shoveled a good amount of dirt into the hole; to stop it up. The cousins meticulously gassed and filled in every rat hole except for two, one at the front and one at the back of the barn. Despite their diligence, they had tarried longer than expected, and the gasoline vapors had spread all throughout the rats' tunnel maze.

They stood at the first open hole making a considerable racket stomping on the ground in order to drive the rats out of their underground complex.

The plan was to force the rats to evacuate out of the hole at the back of the barn and into the small field where there stood about ten acres of feed corn that had been left to dry on the stalk. The corn had already begun to dry out and had turned brown.

"Go stand behind the barn with this garden hoe," said Pink, "If any rats try to escape, you whack 'em with that hoe."

"Okay," replied 'Lij.

"Are you ready?" Pink yelled from the front of the barn.

"Go ahead," hollered Elijah.

Without knowing that the maze was now filled with volatile gas vapors, Pink reached into his pocket and produced a match. Lighting it off the heel of his boot, he lit the cloth on the end of the stick. He let the torch catch fire good, reached down, and touched it to the entrance of the rat hole.

Once in a great while, things happen so fast and with such violence that we struggle to catch up and realize we are in real trouble.

As soon as the gasoline vapors ignited, an underground explosion resulted that shook the ground with considerable force and produced a muffled boom that startled both Pink and 'Lij.

"God dang!" yelled 'Lij.

In a panic, Pink shot around to the back of the barn just in time to see three of the rats propelled out of the other rat hole like cannonballs. Two of the rats were deceased and the third rat was on fire. The fiery rodent took off through the cornfield and as he scurried through the dried corn, he lit it aflame as he went.

"Good Lord!" yelled Pink. "Get that rat!"

Pink took off his jacket and went to work trying to beat the fire out, while Elijah went after the rat with a garden hoe chopping and cursing.

After a few frantic moments, the fiery rat was dead and the corn crop saved. Pink and 'Lij then spent a considerable amount of time trying to mask the evidence of the burnt corn.

"You drag me into more trouble than I can shake a stick at, Pink," shouted 'Lij. "You've got to be the trouble-makin'est boy in the county!"

Pink laughed and replied, "But just think of the stories we'll tell someday."

"If they don't write 'em on our gravestones!" quipped an angry Elijah.

Chapter 27

As You Like It

Recess after lunchtime was a welcomed reprieve from the long periods students were expected to keep still at their desks. It seemed like the boys benefited most from the opportunity to run around, play catch, or engage in horseplay. Pink was no exception. He was a bit more than average height and weight for his age, and he was fairly strong and tenacious. When he set his mind to do something, he would stay with it until it was finished or he nearly died trying.

It was late May and the last day of school. The majority of the eighth grade students would not go on to attend high school. Most boys would simply go on to work either on the family farm, in mills, or in the coalmines.

Pink had not yet decided on whether he would attend high school. His mother and father had encouraged him to do whatever he wanted regarding the matter, but Pink was unsure.

A lot depended on Charley Aleshire. One reason Pink had

not decided is that neither had Charley. It was a sure bet though that if Charlotte Aleshire continued on to high school, Pink would too.

After a hearty lunch of ham and mashed potatoes with gravy, the students were outside for recess.

Most of the girls were talking and jumping rope, while the boys were chasing one another, wrestling, and playing catch.

Butch Cole was a couple of years older than Pink but a grade behind him. Being older in the seventh grade gave Butch a chip on his shoulder. He was supposed to have graduated eighth grade by now but had failed a few grades and found himself at an age that should have commanded the respect of the younger boys but didn't.

The younger boys didn't dislike Butch because he'd been held back in school, they didn't like him because he was mean. He was just plain mean. He once found some rotten bird eggs in a nest by the lunchroom and threw them at another student.

Pink and 'Lij were tossing a milk carton they had filled with gravel and taped up. Bending over with his left leg out behind him, Elijah wound up like Carl Mays and let the milk carton fly. Pink had a piece of an old mop handle that he and the other boys kept stashed in a boxwood bush, near the door to the lunchroom. He waited for the milk carton, whirling the bat behind his shoulder.

As the carton sped toward Pink, Butch Cole appeared in front of him and swatted it to the ground. He snatched it up and ran off with it.

"Hey, bring that back!" hollered 'Lij.

Butch laughed and threw the carton as far as he could away from 'Lij and Pink.

"Go get it, if you want it so bad," he yelled back as he walked away, now disinterested.

Elijah was furious. Butch was always doing something to ruin everyone's fun. Once, he even used his pocket knife to let the air out of the only football the school owned, simply because he was too clumsy to catch it.

"You ain't got the sense God gave a mule!" shouted 'Lij.

Butch turned back to look at Elijah.

"Take that back!" he demanded.

'Lij grit his teeth and shouted, "Never, you cabbage-headed oaf!"

Butch started toward 'Lij in a march. His fists were already clinched, and his face had reddened noticeably.

Pink darted over and stood in front of his cousin. He put both hands out in front to signal the bully to stop.

"Looky here, Butch, we don't want no trouble with you. I'll fetch the milk carton," said Pink nodding back at Elijah. "We just want to play our baseball game in peace is all."

Butch had already seen red, and it would be near impossible to stop him now. Of all the boys in the junior high school, he was the toughest. He was real stupid, but he was real big too, and when it comes to fisticuffs— big and stupid are a dangerous combination.

"You get outta my way, Pinky! I got business with 'Lij, not you," grunted Butch.

Pink held his ground. Butch stopped and was now standing only a foot or so away from Pink. He pointed a finger in Pink's face, nearly touching his nose, and said, "Step aside, boy, or I'll stomp you down to a mud hole."

"You know I can't do that, Butch. 'Lij is my kin. If you fight him, you gotta fight me too," replied Pink.

"Suit yourself," came Butch's response.

He drew back a hand to hit Pink, but before he could deliver the blow, Pink shouted, "But wait! Before you hit me, you need to think about how much of my blood you're about to get all over them brand new shoes of yours."

Butch stopped and looked down at his feet. Sure enough, he was wearing his new Sunday shoes. They were tan suede with black saddles on the sides. They had been a birthday present from his grandpa and he was mighty proud of them.

Putting his hand down to his side, he began to laugh. He laughed so heartily that he forgot all about the names Elijah had called him. He turned to walk away— stopping only to bend over and clutch his now aching sides.

"C'mon, let's go!" shouted 'Lij, and the pair ran back inside the school building.

Sitting down with the rest of their classmates, Pink and 'Lij exchanged a glance acknowledging how close they had come to getting a real beating from Butch.

When the school day was over and after the bell had rung, Mrs. Lowell excused the class and collected the short essays she'd assigned the students to write after recess. They were to detail, as much as possible, each of their plans for the summer break and whether they would be attending high school.

Pink was near the back of the line, and as he handed in his paper, she smiled and said, "Young man, would you mind waiting after class for just a few minutes? I have something you might find interesting."

Pink stepped aside, to let the others pass, and said, "Yes, Ma'am."

When all the other students had left the room, Mrs. Lowell walked over to her desk, opened a drawer, and from it produced a small brown book. She waved it in her hand signifying that it was something special, just for Pink.

She handed it to him and said, "I wanted to lend you this book to read. I think you will enjoy it immensely. It's a play called *As You Like It*."

Reaching out, Pink took the book and looked it over.

It was an old book. Its cover was worn and tattered. The binding was barely intact. Pink took the book from Mrs. Lowell. "Thank you," he said. He opened it to the title page. "*1880?*" he thought. Pink looked up at Mrs. Lowell and remarked about the book's age.

"It *is* quite old but not as old as the original," she explained. "William Shakespeare wrote this play over three hundred years ago, and it is still some of the best literature ever written," she added.

"You don't mind if I take it home?" asked Pink.

"Not at all, young man. I trust you to see that it doesn't become worse for wear," she assured, "Maybe you can just return it to me in the fall."

Pink grinned, he knew what his teacher was up to. She had spoken to him many times during the year to encourage him to go on to the ninth grade. "What's it about?" he asked.

Mrs. Lowell thought a moment, and smiled, "It's a story about betrayal, forgiveness, finding true love, redemption, and coming to terms with your circumstances. We don't always get a say in the fix we are in, but in this play, Mr. Shakespeare demonstrates that we may indeed have a say in how we react."

Pink smiled. That Mrs. Lowell thought enough to keep him after class and share the book made him feel important and smart. He thumbed the pages and put it in his pocket. Picking up his books by the leather strap with which they were bound and slinging them over his back, he started out of the door.

"Pink," called his teacher, "I think you are a very special young man. You have gifts that deserve cultivation. I do hope you will consider continuing your education in high school."

He smiled and nodded his head. It was a lot to think about. Eighth grade was as far as anyone in his family had ever gone in school and Pink really didn't see a need to go any further. Still, Mrs. Lowell's encouragement carried weight with him.

"I'll think about over the summer," he said, "Well, it's a good long walk home. I best get started."

"Bless you, Pink Malone," responded the teacher.

Mrs. Lowell watched him until he was nearly out of sight. Of all the students in her class, she considered Pink to be the most gifted in a special way. He wasn't the brightest student academically, by any stretch. Pink never got the best marks on tests. He rarely diagramed sentences correctly and his grammar was often atrocious, but there was something unique about the way he saw the world and especially people.

Mrs. Lowell had taught Pink in 7th grade English and now in her 8th grade Literature and English classes. She had noticed early on that Pink saw the world in a series of tiny pauses. He was never in a hurry to get on to the next task and miss whatever was going on in the moment.

At times, she became frustrated with Pink because she assumed he was just daydreaming or distracted, and in a way she was right. Pink was fascinated by people and treasures found hidden in nature.

She knew about the way he had come into the Malone family. By the time Pink was around eight years of age, everyone knew that he had been taken in by CD and Leola Malone.

Some treated him like an outsider on account of his being adopted, but others, like Nelda Lowell, saw him as a wonderful creature with many special gifts.

As Mrs. Lowell watched him from the doorway of the junior high building, she saw Pink stop walking and divert into the tall grass, on the side of the road.

Her husband, who taught arithmetic at the school, noticed her standing in the hall entrance. Curiosity got the better of him, and he moved towards the doorway.

Walking up behind her, he said, "Loitering after school hours is not permitted, miss."

Recognizing his voice, Nelda turned and greeted him with a smile. He put his arm around her and strained to see what had her attention fixed so. "What are you looking at?" he asked.

She smiled and with her best teacher voice replied, "At what are you looking? You mean."

"Yes, I am sorry, I forgot *to whom* I was speaking," he replied.

Nelda laughed and patted him on the chest. She turned back to see if she could still see Pink in the distance. He emerged from the grass, holding a large wild carrot.

"I would give almost anything to know how that boy's mind works," she said softly.

"What do you mean?" asked Jon.

Nelda looked up at him and grinned. She opened her mouth to speak but instead, just put her head on his shoulder and gave a relieved sigh.

Jon held her close and stroked her hair. He could sense when Nelda had given part of her heart to a student. It was a trait in her that had first attracted him.

"You have a beautiful heart and you're a wonderful teacher. I do love you so!" he said. "What is it about Pink that has you so intent on helping him?" he inquired.

She pulled away to look into Jon's eyes and said, "He sees the world differently than us. He sees something that I think we all miss. Sometimes..." she hesitated for a second, and then continued, "Sometimes, I think he hears a song playing all around us that we cannot. It's as if he's being called to a dance."

THE END...

About the Author

 Bill Winn grew up just a few feet above sea level on a small farm down east in North Carolina. He's a son, brother, cousin, nephew, husband, father, pastor, friend, and author. He pastors at Grace Communion Hanover in Mechanicsville, VA.

About the Illustrator

Alisa Lincoln is an artist, writer, speaker, creative encourager and lover of beauty.

"Beauty is at the very core of who we are, our true identity. It's essential, far more than we have ever realized." ~ Alisa Lincoln

You can learn more about Alisa at <u>beautyrestores.com</u>

Glossary

Lay-by: Lay-by is a stage of plant growth when row croppers are able to till the soil between the rows before the plants' canopies close in and make it impossible to hill the rows without damaging the plants. During lay-by family members would collect, along with their mules and plows, on various farms to help till the rows before the plants matured.

School Hack: Early form of a school bus originally a horse drawn wagon with wooden benches. Later hacks were motorized but remained open air for many years.

Under-drawers: Underwear, under-britches.

Dinner: The afternoon meal and usually the heaviest meal of the day.

Catchin': just means contagious. If a virulent illness was going around folks would say, "It's real catchin'."

Gondola: In railroad terms, it is a railcar that has sides but an open top. A high-side gondola has, well, high sides.

Short-leg: A chicken thigh. Most folks forget that the thigh is part of the chicken's leg... it's just the short part.

Tintype: Early photograph.

Uncouth: Crude, unrefined, without good manners.

Peashooter: A slingshot.

Brimstone: Sulfur.

Rabbit Gum: A rabbit trap traditionally made from a hollowed out Sweetgum tree log.

Fit to be Tied: The state of being so angry it nearly warrants being tied up.

Moving Picture Shows: Movies.

Brogans: High-topped leather lace-up work boots, usually brown.

Worried Sick to Death: Being so worried as to cause illness.

Cribbing: Stacks of timbers used to shore up loads or sloughing soil.

Bit: (in money) A bit is 12 ½ cents or one eighth of a dollar. Two bits is one quarter dollar.

Lollygag: To dawdle, go slow as to waste time.

'est: Added to any word to turn it into a superlative adjective.

Lollygaggin'est: One who lollygags the most.

Batty: crazy, To drive one batty is to drive one crazy.

Parvo: A disease in animals caused by parasitic worms that leaves the animal real skinny.

Crackin' someone's corn: to tease in good hearted fun.

Alphabetical Order: something the author thought might be fun not to use here.

Made in United States
Troutdale, OR
12/23/2023

16391041R00159